D0906544

THE COLONIAL HOTEL

Also by Jonathan Bennett

Fiction

Entitlement (2008)

Verandah People (2003)

After Battersea Park (2001)

Poetry

Civil and Civic (2011)

Here is my street, this tree I planted (2004)

THE
COLONIAL
HOTEL

a novel

Jonathan Bennett

ECW Press
a misFit book

Published by ECW Press
2120 Queen Street East, Suite 200
Toronto, Ontario, Canada M4E 1E2
416-694-3348 / info@ecwpress.com

This is a work of fiction. Names, characters, places, and incidents either
are the product of the author's imagination or are used fictitiously, and
any resemblance to actual persons, living or dead, business establishments, events, or locales is entirely coincidental.

LIBRARY AND ARCHIVES CANADA CATALOGUING IN PUBLICATION

Bennett, Jonathan, 1970-, author
The Colonial Hotel : a novel / Jonathan Bennett.

ISBN 978-1-77041-178-4 (BOUND)
ALSO ISSUED AS: 978-1-77090-518-4 (PDF); 978-1-77090-519-1 (EPUB)

I. Title.
PS8553.E534C64 2014   C813'.6   C2013-907757-X   C2013-907758-8

Editor for the press: Michael Holmes
Cover design: Natalie Olsen, Kisscut Design
Cover photo: Gräfin. / photocase.com
Author photo: Rebekah Littlejohn
Production and typesetting: Lynn Gammie
Printing: Friesens 1 2 3 4 5

The publication of *The Colonial Hotel* has been generously supported by
the Canada Council for the Arts which last year invested $157 million to
bring the arts to Canadians throughout the country, and by the Ontario
Arts Council (OAC), an agency of the Government of Ontario, which
last year funded 1,681 individual artists and 1,125 organizations in 216
communities across Ontario for a total of $52.8 million. We also acknowl-
edge the financial support of the Government of Canada through the
Canada Book Fund for our publishing activities, and the contribution of
the Government of Ontario through the Ontario Book Publishing Tax
Credit and the Ontario Media Development Corporation.

PRINTED AND BOUND IN CANADA

For my daughter, Ivy

PART ONE: PARIS & HELEN

Since my eyes have been outraged by your letter,
there is now no glory in silence.
—Ovid, *Heroides, XVII: Helen to Paris*

Paris

THE COLONIAL HOTEL WAS PAINTED white and had a wrought iron fence covered with bougainvillea. I sat at an open window in the café on its main floor. In the street local youths on spluttering mopeds or older men on bicycles swerved between pedestrians and donkeys. I was watching for Helen. Every few minutes a convoy of three or four trucks carrying loads of aid rations rumbled past, bound for the mouth of the swollen river, the bridge, border, and the refugee camp beyond.

The bones of the city's architecture were European. The last half-century had seen makeshift shops and houses rise or fall—the new growing next to, or over the top of, the old. From my seat in the hotel's café I saw bullet holes in the façades, bills advertising local music or foreign films alongside party propaganda posters. The few recently constructed buildings had corrugated metal roofs with walls of cinderblock. The trees in the park across the road were stumpy with dull-coloured leaves, except the ones that bore the orange-red, sweet fruit—the name of which I never learned.

My daughter, can you see me sitting there easily enough? Can you imagine how the sun warmed my face while I read the local English-language newspaper? I remember that morning exactly, the diesel smell, a lizard climbing the wall of the hotel, the bougainvillea, the feel of the damp paper in the humidity.

I found foreign newspapers beguiling. The words before me on the page were the same ones I'd always known. They meant what they always had. Yet here, just as in the other countries where I'd practised medicine, I had expected historical hatred and the cycle of revenge between opposing polit-ical factions to be obvious. Isn't that the story we've come to know? But where was the evidence? If there *were* signals on the street corners or in the newsprint before me, they were coded in signs meant only for the locals. Or was I blind?

I had pursued Helen through a growing list of poor countries. They were maimed by war, plagued by acts of God. Some were simply lost regions, having been renamed, split, joined, or annexed from our global mind. As part of a team of freelance clinicians we provided medical aid. Helen and I landed on improbable airstrips, climbed into ancient jeeps. Our team would wait whole days at dusty, hot bus terminals, find ourselves eating or drinking in dank establishments with worn-felt pool tables and local men looking for work, or drink, or women. Our safety was always at some risk. We were obvious and exposed. But despite this there was the rush of constant movement, of oncoming newness. The repetitive and rapid deployment produced in me a numbness to specific locations. The newspapers from each of these countries, when published in English, bled together over time to read as one bleak story, one political struggle, one act of poverty.

They weren't of course. They all differed, in ways major and minor. My daughter, admitting this to you now doesn't please me. I think that Helen and I were just too easily attracted to this organization. It *was* filled with devoted clinicians. We cared only about saving lives. So we chased the fatalities from the next roadside bomb, famine, drought, outbreak, or flood. As medical personnel we were overeager to attempt dramatic interventions on the all-but-dead, the pulled-out bodies, the blown-apart, and too-seriously diseased. We were often ill-equipped and, it seemed to me, inexperienced.

On whose authority did we operate? For many of my colleagues, it was God's work. A simple, discrete answer for everything. Helen's faith guided her. In this way, she led me.

Yet, from the beginning I struggled. There was often no one left to stay and provide follow-up care, to ensure these lives were worth living. Our group worked around the clock, urging each other on, treating in the midst of gunfire, betting bluff against the very real circumstances. We moved on and left the pain management, the healing, the aftermath, to God, or chance, or maybe both.

That morning in the Colonial Hotel's café I had opted for coffee. While I had developed a taste for Fanta—seemingly always available and safer than local water—this place was upscale and reserved for foreigners. Helen and I were drawn to its luxuries a second time, as respite from what we had witnessed in the camp. I savoured a good coffee. There were, from time to time, these recuperative days when Helen and I would take a room in as nice a hotel as a place had to offer, and hole up. I would shave, wash, and scrape myself clean. I would launder, or even buy a dress shirt if I could, doing the buttons up casually. I would read a local newspaper.

It was time off and a chance to look the other way, or else pause and feel momentarily righteous about ourselves. Yes, my daughter, we did lapse into self-congratulation. When Helen would comment on how I had diagnosed this or acted quickly to save that, the world dissolved around me. I had never felt stronger, more powerful, in all my life. The absolute right of religion, when delivered by the likes of Helen, made me feel immortal.

That morning, and the events that followed, happened years ago. Memory is an unpredictable and inaccurate shot, but I will aim to set this down honestly for you. I will also try to protect those who committed crimes during the war—or those who did nothing to prevent them—by changing their names. I must leave this country as unidentifiable as I can, to spare everyone here the indignity of having me record their struggles in a language they don't use. This isn't evidence. I'll leave justice, or reconciliation, for other people.

My purpose is simple. This is my story, that's all. I want to write it out for you, my daughter, to have and to keep.

My name is Paris. I am forty-three years old. I was a physician. I live in this hillside village. I am dying.

I recall a conversation that Helen and I had had the evening before, how everyone was talking about the rainy season *being in the air*.

Where else would it be, she'd laughed.

On the main street, the original buildings still

stood and had been mostly kept up, housing a foreign development bank and an outpost of the government's agriculture department. I'd said to Helen that I'd half expected to see some throwback colonial administrator with a waxed moustache come striding out from the arched promenade wearing jodhpurs.

This isn't a movie set, she'd said, plainly. Helen was like that—lighthearted one minute, serious the next.

A café au lait please, and a brioche, I told the server. While I waited, I saw two half-dead dogs, ribcages heaving, tongues lolling, hunting hopelessly for food. One had blood caked onto its hind leg. The morning damp was keeping the dust down at least. I remember these details easily. These are hours I have replayed many times, searching my memory for scraps I might have missed.

There Helen was across the street, talking to a vendor who sold leather goods, belts and wallets.

Daughter, you might rightly ask how we could reconcile enjoying such pleasure given its close proximity to the human suffering found in the camps that we had just left behind. The answer, as I saw it then, was that we were not at this work for the short term. We purchased our way out from underneath the poverty that weighed down this country, and all countries like it, to remain sane and safe. It was essential for us to continue at this work month in, month out.

Helen and I had come to accept our station in these places. Staying at the only affluent hotel was expected. To forgo the status and safety it afforded would be to risk becoming, or appearing to become, a political player. Even if creating political change was morally right, doing so would have placed us in danger. Our reasons for being there were medical. We treated only the effects.

The gaps in this logic seem larger to me now.

As a nurse, Helen took the dangerous assignments seriously and willingly. She went deep into whichever continent needed her, as determined by others at our organization's headquarters. As a physician, my skills and knowledge were in demand—but in truth I had little driving me other than the desire to follow Helen.

Daughter, I hope you don't think of me as too simple.

Helen was haggling for something—perhaps a present for me? I admit to hoping so. I returned to the smell of newsprint, adopting an absorbed expression once I saw her approaching.

Why do you always sit in the sun? Helen asked. She smiled faintly. You're like an old dog. Her eye caught sight of the lizard climbing farther up the wall.

She had bought a suede bookmark and pulled out a paperback, slipping it inside. Her lip curled in the way it did when she was thinking. She was effortlessly beautiful. Her arms were tanned and strong from the work, especially the recent long days at the camp. All that water we'd carried. Had the three peacekeeping soldiers not arrived, would we still have been treading that path to and from the truck, water sloshing out of discarded gasoline canisters? She had on her travel outfit, the blue jeans and slim white T-shirt. She was readying to leave here. From her pocket Helen pulled a printout of an email that she'd just received from a colleague who'd been reassigned several weeks back. The printer paper was the old kind, with the perforation and small holes down each side.

We need you badly here, she read aloud. *It's worsening each day. We are getting no sleep. See if they will transfer you and Paris—some of the other girls too.* I could tell by the tone of her delivery that Helen was feeling the lure of new work, a different, equally unmanageable, horror. *Please ask Paris to lean on the organization, pressure the executive director.*

She looked at me, not needing to ask again in her own words, knowing I would oblige. Even here, the medical hierarchy lives, a physician's influence can tip the balance of any set of scales.

May I have some? Helen asked, and broke off a piece of brioche.

I bought it for you, I said.

At the next table was a woman I had not seen before. I remember her easily. But why? Her face, haircut, mannerisms? She applied lipstick, looked at herself in a compact mirror and snapped it closed impatiently. Helen did not wear makeup. Brushing her hair and washing her face were all she required.

How is your leg? I asked Helen. I had put four stitches in her thigh at the camp the previous week. She'd cut herself on the tailgate of a truck. I'd boiled water to wash out the cut then sutured it as she sang her national anthem through clenched teeth. She gave up on the singing and did not cry but rather moaned in guttural bursts of controlled pain until I'd finished. No infection developed. What were the chances?

Before I began this work with Helen I'd had just a few years behind me working as an emergency department physician. I'd been following no path beyond paying off student loans, still enjoying my unencumbered authority as a doctor both at and away from the hospital. I turned my back on that life when I fell in love with Helen.

Across the café, expatriates were seated in clusters. A few were aid workers we knew, or knew of, or else they were bank employees, or with the oil company that was test drilling in the country's north. Each read or wrote postcards, or laughed together in the bright and familiar vernacular of home, or daydreamed in silence, or ate and drank having just returned from work, or greedily sought news of the next flight out or details of who might be arriving on the next one in.

The sun was on Helen's skin too. It was on her face. She smiled then. It lit her light brown hair.

Let's go down to the capital tomorrow, Helen said.

We should get a bus, I said. I've heard the road the trucks use through the southern mountains is not safe for cars.

If you like, she said. Paris, she added, I was sick again this morning.

Can I do anything?

We had been back and forth—the capital on the South Coast, to this town, then to the camp—only to retrace our steps several times now. That morning, on the only computer in the hotel, I'd waited as it dialled up a connection. I had quickly typed an overdue letter, then emailed it off. I'd finally ended my leave-of-absence from the hospital to do humanitarian work by resigning outright. It was inconceivable that I would ever leave Helen.

We talked properly then. Helen spoke of missing a number of the camp children—the loneliest ones she spoke of by name. I saw that our departure was not just due to the pull of a new assignment. Helen needed to get farther away. If she stayed she would become too attached. She knew she must stave off that ache to give more to those she'd already nursed so intimately. The ache happened when she stopped, when she could think. If she didn't leave today, tomorrow she would be aboard a morning convoy, back into the camp's dusty mouth—an open mouth of sores, silent, rotting, and dry from months of screaming.

=

Helen

I SAW THE DAYBREAK AGAIN. The sun hung on the horizon for that impatient moment. There it was, its thick forearms of light scooping up the sky, me along with it. Why must you get me up so early, child? I made myself a tea and am sitting by the window of our room. We are back in the Colonial Hotel, Paris and I. Here on the second floor. The cup is bone china. I love the word *porcelain*—so pretty. The morning light has no heat. The damp of this morning is chilling me. I know it's old-fashioned to do this, to write in a diary in longhand. But it's the only way. So I sit here. Drink tea, write to you as I have promised, my little one.

You are a peanut. The size of one, I mean.

Has history itself dissolved? This window looks out along the old part of the town. The slums are behind us and out of sight. I watch the goings-on, an ox pulling a cart to morning market. The man driving the cart is walking alongside, lost in time. Two women, one short, one tall, carry water in earthen vessels. They gossip. Their laughter comes easily. It trickles through my window in threads of melody.

As a girl I woke early. Still in pyjamas I would sit on the back step and count the ocean waves, one-two-three. Or watch the joggers huffing past on the esplanade. Spot cats finishing up their prowling. Wait for the surfers to paddle out over the dark peaks, disappearing into the troughs.

Peanut, the careful business of truth telling is best done in the early morning. Do wake up from time to time and take part. Life's all so sound. But only on the surface. The orderly way—it's how the world behaves during the daytime. Even in the camp. Rules and order seep into life there too. We need rules. But how *appropriate* we all are to one another. The lies are wearying after a time. Even though I'm tired now, I need the early morning. While there is still some dark to be had, the truth is freer. To be thought, yes, or spoken, or written like this. Paris is twitching in his dreams.

A boy dribbles a soccer ball down the street. It is a shiny ball. Perhaps the ball is stolen? He controls it near to his feet. So attractive an object that he dare only play with it this early, when it is safe to do so.

This boy is languid, if that is the right word. He is performing for an audience inside his own mind, an imaginary announcer describing his talents to the crowd. None other than his admiring self.

Paris talked about the way boys do this. At the camp we'd both noticed a similar-aged boy. We'd treated him for an infected eye, purple and angry. He was playing soccer, yes seriously, but with no ball at all. Paris said that many young boys do this kind of play acting. Pretending that they are exceptional.

Boys are like the men they become. They have insides that are as sensitive to burning as the fairest skin.

Are girls so different? Wanting our efforts recognized, our abilities applauded by crowds of unknowns? Yes, I think so.

Here is some truth: boys want to hear they are gifted, girls that they are a gift.

My baby. Peanut. Do you know the first time I knew you would be made? Paris had only been with us a short time. He was stitching up a long gash in a woman's leg, caused by her husband's machete. We were in a former school building of mud bricks and sheet-metal walls with no roof. A generator motored away outside, keeping the lights on. It was the only modern assistance we had. Supplies were dwindling. The truck from the capital would not arrive for another day. I remember all this. Paris looked at me and said this young woman could not wait and so we worked on her together. I was the only one free. I shared his, and God's, belief that she was worth treating immediately, even under such duress.

Paris sutured her so carefully. I can only imagine that if she is still alive, has not been finished off by her husband's machete, that she shows off her beautiful, disappearing scar to any woman in the village who might wish to peek at it. She puts to shame their keloid gnarls and angry disfigured pits of skin.

In Paris, I saw God at work. The dignity and certainty of a good man dedicated to the lambs. The thin lines around his eyes were earned from long periods of concentration and seriousness. As an emotional person, he presented as a man partly erased by genuine dedication to scientific method and the plight of others. I saw a person who donated to the world his entire mind, a doctor capable of retaining vast amounts of information, a man with kind, sure hands. He knew the burden of what we were trying to do, all of this madness. And almost because of that, as he stitched, came the first idea of you I'd ever had.

I allowed Paris to become my lover because I wanted you. I needed you.

I trained to be a nurse to keep pain close. Yet I soon found that the profession (as practised day-to-day in a general hospital) wasn't nearly intense or trying enough. Mr. So-and-So's saggy bottom that needed changing. Lecherous old doctors. Hours spent entering every scrap of pointless detail into a computer. Lecherous young doctors. In the final hours of a matriarch's life, her family declaring the sad, emotional wars fought over a whole lifetime permanently unresolved. *At least you have a mother*, I'd mostly wanted to spit at them.

I was a bird with new feathers. Why did the sky not open up before me?

I felt that I must make it do so. This was the urge I followed, my baby. The feeling that only the young have, that they are destined for greatness if they could only free themselves of their past, or that they are invincible and there is no one else quite like them. Another morning truth: delusional uniqueness—a condition that resolves untreated with age.

Is this why I ran away and find myself sitting, writing in a diary at this window? Because I wanted freedom and was naive? Is this why I went nursing in war zones: to ensure the pain I had about me was not bourgeois, democratic, and mediocre, but rather was devastatingly poor, lawless, and catastrophic?

No, it was more than simple youthful adventure that drove me here. I understand it now as a kind of mental illness—a way to avoid having love for others, a way to keep people at a distance. Either literally through all this reckless travel. Or by insisting on professional boundaries. The selflessness others saw in me was, of course, calculated selfishness of the worst kind. I wasn't giving myself to the care of others. I knew, more or less, what I was doing. I was forgoing my life to pursue God, in a kind of living martyrdom—a state of emotional numbness. Some choose drugs, others a bullet I suppose. Don't think I didn't consider the various other options as a teenager. In the end, I chose high-risk nursing. This is my daily overdose attempt. My open cry for God's love. It keeps me free and others away. See, peanut, the truth speaks at dawn.

Will you be born in a tent at night on the edge of a desert? I can picture you coming in waves, the heat leaching out of the sand about me. The night cold swelling in a sudden shock. Above the stars are all out, pricks of light that burst with each of my contractions, I squeeze handfuls of sand and rock, then a single star becomes a focal point as I push, crushing earth to dust between fingers and palm. I reach for Paris but not even he can help me here. You come with a fight, the Milky Way smearing. Propped against the coarse bark of a tree I try to control myself to the end, in case last-minute refusal might be my first and final act of motherhood. But the more you come, the further I get lost. I curse Paris under each breath. *You*

did this. You left her in me; now she is leaving me.
Everybody leaves me.

What else do I imagine? Do I see my nursing colleagues close by? We have been through so much together—famine, flood, war. We have witnessed so many moments of death, consoled those still sentenced to live. We are bound. But as I push you into this world, all I see is a lone midwife from a local village. There is no one else in attendance. Has a bomb gone off an hour earlier? Did my colleagues say, *We'll be back*, climbing into jeeps? *Breathe*, they sing together, *breathe.*

I am going to refuse to tell them the name of your father. Paris—there he sleeps so soundly—will be the one most suspected, of course. But were there other men? Trysts, affairs? Where do I go, when I do not go with him? They have always wondered. Their conjecture will be restless.

Why will I not tell them? We are sisters! They will plead, over beers at a restaurant on a week off in a city, the name of which I will never recall. I will sit there eating steamed fish wrapped in a banana leaf with rice—oh that I will remember, so good—but I will maintain my silence, withhold the story.

Increasingly it will become clear to them I cannot be trusted.

You might think this hard of me, or them.

Ours is a sorority of survival though. Solidarity

and absolute trust, the kind of honour code you might expect among front line soldiers going into battle. But this was what was demanded of each nurse. In unison, we would not break, not be weakened. There are interloping men of course. Doctors such as Paris come and go. Taking pieces of each of us with them, back to their lives, their wives. There are other NGO workers stationed at a camp, or the one-night stand with a local man met on a day off that starts as no more than a smile across a restaurant. If we open our legs, it is only to feel something—*a soothing, a hurt*—to have or to lose even the texture of power, for a precious few moments.

There. See. I *am* alive.

Paris stirs under the mosquito net. He is a decent, kind man. But I have not fallen in love with him yet. I am sorry to write so starkly. For your sake I hope to, I do.

I wonder if you will have my eyes?

Will we travel about together? How can I continue working in the field? You will be in harm's way, just *in the way*, despite my best intentions. The others will assist as they can for a while but in having you I will fail these women and the organization's mission. Rightly, they will see my bond with you as unbreakable. How can I give episodic care to many when you will require total care from me? Milk from my breast. Crying. Sicknesses. I know they will grow to hate me for having you. For the first time in my life, the choices before me will really matter to me—because it will matter even more to another person I love: you.

I will get us out of here, of this life, to protect you. Paris will understand. He will follow and keep us safe. Yes, it's clear. This is the journey before us now.

You are only a peanut, but you have already begun to change me.

———

Paris

THE FIRST SOLDIER THROUGH THE hotel café's door banged his machete blade three times against the metal pillar by the glass pastry display. I caught Helen's eye. There was urgency in her look. The soldier spoke hurried words in the northern dialect that sounded angry and directive. If any of the foreigners in the room understood what he asked of us, none let on. Again he rapped his machete. A man in a group toward the front raised both his arms, palms facing forward. The rest of his group followed his lead, lifting their hands in the air. With compliance as the only available choice, table after table did the same.

Helen then mouthed a local word. It was one I knew, but had never said myself. It was the word the children in the camps cried out at night, as their dreams turned sour. It was the word their mothers used as a curse or a way to damn the moment, or person. It was the word that meant *them*, the people from over the mountains to the north. Those who did all this. Those at fault. Those responsible for raping their sisters and daughters. Those who took their land and killed their husbands. It was an acidic word that named both a people and, at the same time, said *I accuse*. I had learned this word, this word for *them*, within a day of my arrival. And I knew what it meant as it soundlessly formed in Helen's mouth. Our hands were now in the air. Other soldiers entered, ordering and gesturing.

I had also learned that the local word meaning blindness was the same as the word for a foreign person with white skin. To them, we look all the same. The term, it had been explained to us, meant literally *erased by the light*. We were white on white—ghostlike. It was an old, weighty word, and we heard it daily. It had been whispered throughout the camps, as we walked past women warming themselves at fires by night, or in the streets of the capital as we passed bars where the men drank and smoked or chewed in the afternoons. The children worked the word into songs in ways they believed were clever enough that we would not know or understand.

This word, now being thrown about by the soldiers, was spoken differently, in an accent or a regional dialect. Helen and I picked it out easily. The tone they used was the same.

Sources speculate that they will soon cross the river. This was a line I had just read in the newspaper.

Khaki shirts. Black boots. The sweat and smoky smell of fiery, rural men, made fit from the harvest but left poor after the southern government's tariffs. I knew the basic facts from the newspapers, from camp gossip, about a rising discontent in the North.

Sources confirm that northern recruitment continues to be strong. Signing up is especially popular with young men from towns negatively affected by the government's crop taxes enacted in the last budget.

Why did this report not immediately resonate with me? The shifting politics had not been properly monitored by either prosperous governments or by our own organization. How could I have failed to recognize such a warning? More soldiers strode in through the front door while others blocked the back.

My daughter, the events of the next twenty minutes are not always clear in my memory. I recall the soldiers pointing and ordering. Helen pivoted away from me, and spoke to the woman at the next table. I didn't catch what she said. Then, in a voice that sounded annoyed, the woman responded by saying something like: why didn't we know this was happening today? From her accent, I knew she was from back home.

He said I was a day late for our meeting, Helen then replied, all but under her breath.

They'll press on toward the camps, said the woman.

Down the street bullets cracked out erasing all other sound. I smelled smoke. I felt faint and colours separated, returning to their primary roots, filling my field of vision. We were ushered out of the café in a line of the blind—they shouted the word at us again and again. Their machetes glinted in the sun. The street was empty of traffic and people. Only the leather vendor was still out, standing beside his stall, watching, a lone witness.

The woman from the café was ahead of us. Both she and Helen were staring at the leather vendor. I ask myself still, did they seem less scared than me?

We were all taken. They arrested us. We were abducted.

Over there was the bougainvillea, a lizard, an unfinished coffee, a picked-at brioche. My newspaper was left open in the sun. These details remain fixed in my mind, as if I might return to the hotel today and find everything as we'd left it, untouched. I was wearing a freshly ironed cotton dress shirt that was white with pale green stripes. Helen led me by the hand as we formed a line and boarded a large military transport truck.

The jolt of the flatbed shook us forcibly. We were livestock, the town's colonial buildings receding in flashes through breaks in the oily canvas covering the back of the truck. We drove until midday, diesel fumes, dust in our mouths, lurching. No one much spoke—except for a woman who muttered in French, repeating the Lord's Prayer. Helen's hand was still gripping onto my own. For a time she leaned over and had a whispered conversation with the other woman. I could not hear the words.

Does she know what's going on? I asked Helen.

My daughter, I have to explain that in the years that followed, to the core of my being, I stayed clutching onto Helen's hand. I denied those bare threads of evidence. That a few simple words exchanged with an apparent stranger could suggest she was other than Helen, a nurse—the woman I loved. How could a person known intimately be something other? So I held onto her hand, in my mind, always pushing away any suggestion that there was more I did not know. Never asking the question, was she not wholly honest? Were there two Helens?

Daughter, these are the crimes I witnessed that day. It was long ago. It was during a civil war. I describe them knowing how horrible they are, that these are not the pictures and memories with which a father should burden his daughter. I do not judge. I know the whereabouts of a few of these men, and many like them, today. Some are good fathers, or else they work hard and pray. Others still are no longer here, having started new lives afresh in other parts of the country, or elsewhere around the world. Maybe you pass them on the street on the way to school or eat next to them at a restaurant. You wouldn't know. Who am I to present my feeble memories as evidence? And what if I am biased? Possibly my memory is faulty.

I have reconstructed this day over and over, for so many years. Have the details faded until I have changed them to keep it feeling as fresh as when it first happened? I mustn't think so. I must believe this is what occurred around me. What I cannot say, or explain, is why. Why did my life take this turn? At what precise point did I make the wrong choice? Possibly there are too many moments to choose from.

My daughter, I cannot name these men. Please understand, and share in my attempt at forgiveness. Can we ever appreciate the hurts and injustices that another has experienced? That, in turn, led him to speak or act? Was there ever a true beginning, a first stone cast? I hope for there to be no new violent beginnings. There *can* be ends.

My dearest girl, that day I saw only culmi-
nating pieces, horrible deeds committed against
human sanctity. Sadly, there is still more to come.
That was just one savage day in a decade-long civil
war where two different, ever-advancing scores were
being kept. Today there is peace. There is government. Men work, and women again have children
borne of love. But the paint is fresh on the houses,
as they say here. While the wind blows it dry, please
accept that my writing this must be a subtle exercise
in case it is ever read by someone other than you.

I'll come back, but let me skip ahead because
Helen and I were taken from one another this day. I
can still see Helen searching for my face as the jeep
drove her away. Daughter, you likely ask, what did
my heart say when I lost my lover? That is simple.
It said, *Helen, I am here, love. Over here! Look this way.*

And then? I *will her* to leap from the moving
jeep and fly to me, employing the logic and physics
of unsettled dreams. I imagine us lifting off, and
fleeing this scene, this region, until we reach the
coast where we catch a plane to safety. We are
together then, in a familiar place that is perfectly
ordinary, with families and children, parks, hospitals,
and schools. It is a normal place—where we can
raise you, the child growing in her belly.

Daughter, this is how I know of you: our last
night together, before being arrested and taken from

the hotel's café, Helen came to me in those thick, hotel sheets. She took my hand and placed it on her stomach.

Eventually, we will need to make some plans, she said.

A baby?

It's a girl. She's the size of a peanut.

How could you know this, out here? That it's a girl, I mean.

An old woman at the camp came up to me. I was playing with some children, under that forked fruit tree by the school tent. She said some words in their language and smiled, placing her hand here as I'm doing with you, then on my forehead, like this. I looked at her deeply, Paris. I just knew what she was doing, what she was telling me. One of the youngest girls, the one with the cleft palate, was close by and overheard. She giggled. She said in English, *Girl— she says you have girl baby inside.*

=

Helen

I WOKE STARTLED. IT IS still night and a sliver of moon hangs low in the sky. In the streets below there is a rumble of trucks and cars. It is the sound of fleeing. The people of the city are heading farther south. The roads cannot be safe. We are not yet surrounded but their positions must be growing stronger in the low mountains that lie between here and the capital on the South Coast. Military trucks from the North are arriving hourly, bringing ever more troops and supplies. I am back in the room at the Colonial Hotel, at the same window where I wrote only yesterday morning. It seems weeks ago. I am tired, but my heart races.

Paris's belongings are here. I tore through them earlier tonight. What was I hoping to find? Perhaps just something to focus all this raw emotion I have. At the bottom of his duffel bag of clothes were two books—both that I gave him, Rilke poems and a gag gift, a handbook of slang and swear words from home. I flipped through his photograph album, which he had shown me before. There are a few shots of his father and an aunt, a childhood dog. A picture of a girlfriend he had in university—she is quite pretty but he left her. Apparently his studies took priority. No snaps of himself. In his toiletry kit were the usual items and I'd seen them before. He has an old straight razor that he occasionally uses—his father's. There were some drugs for himself, just in case I suppose—a course of penicillin, various painkillers. He travels lightly in every way.

There's not much to Paris. What's confounding is that for someone so intelligent, so confident and sure-footed, he doesn't have the worldly wounds that would normally be required to make up such a person's stoic character. He's never been in love, before now. Once hurt, a person protects himself. Paris guards nothing.

Gunshots again, they snap and fly off into the night. I am controlling my breathing to stay calm. I can see a car on fire in the distance. The other two women who were released with me are staying in the room next door. I wanted to be alone in a room. Why do I value my privacy more than my safety? It gives me room to pray, yes, but there is something more too. Earlier, downstairs, we found bottles of water and food in the kitchen. The soldiers had been through but had not taken much. The power is out. The old refrigerator was still cool inside. We helped ourselves to yesterday's bread still on the counter, to some local fruit and soft cheese. We drank the last of the raw milk, which was thick, still cool, and delicious. We gathered up whatever else that would keep in a tea towel—the cured meats that hung in the pantry, tins of sardines, a dozen small mangoes. We have enough supplies to last a week if we eat with restraint; however, I expect the Colonel will be back in the morning.

My daughter, despite what I said about not yet loving Paris, tonight I am thinking mostly of him. Is he safe? Surely he knows that if he saves lives they will spare his. I will get word out as soon as I am able. They will know what to do, how to get him back to safety.

We are telling the truth here, right, peanut? This was our agreement.

I make too many agreements. I don't negotiate deals though. Rather, I bind myself to people, or work, or causes, without ever really being definitive or setting limits or boundaries. I know I do this. Yet I continue to act in this way. How? The next step is presented as an extension of what I have already agreed to, so to say no would seem small-minded, arbitrary, or mean. And how do I know that this is not simply God's will at work? So I carry on, the obligations pointing my way forward. I have no overarching plan. I've always been like this; it's who I am. I need to feel attached and purposeful. As a result, I am used as a means to an end. I loathe this about myself, but I don't know how to stop. I apply all my faith. I keep pressing on faster, directly at the nearest danger. Then there is no time for shame. No time for me to simply be here in the moment. Like this. Yes, I hate this. I am doing this for you. I can't even remember the name of this town. It was unpronounceable in any case. I never know where I am led. I just show up and go to work, inject those who scream in pain, change dressings, say happy things to brand new orphans.

My contacts find me. I never look for them. I never know when they will appear. Just that, in each country where I am sent, they find me. They are usually women. They assume occupations such as filmmakers, engineers, foreign workers, or travellers. I feel myself being watched. Sometimes for just an hour, other times for days. Then I am approached. A brief, casual-looking conversation occurs. I say little. I am given instructions. Usually, I am to ask something of someone else. Sometimes it's just the name of, say, a local chief's daughter, or else so-and-so's father. Other times it's the whereabouts of a man's home, or where a person is originally from. The information is never hard to come by. I often ask the patients I treat, work it naturally into conversations if they speak English. Sometimes other aid workers know the answers, especially if they've been in the place for a while. The information is mostly connected to the power structures of the villages, towns, cities, or camps we are in. I can't always get what they want. Then they just ask for something else, or disappear into the crowd. They are always foreigners, never locals. Once there was a woman from my own country. She was the only one who ever looked at me with the faintest bit of kindness or interest.

I am not a spy. I wish it were that glamorous. I don't really know what I am.

Once, I had a dream about a thistle. In my dream the thistle was growing out of my thigh. I longed for it to be tugged out. But how? I couldn't get under its roots because they were too deep inside my leg, and I couldn't grab it and tug it out due to the spines. The thistle represented this work I do, I awoke sure of that.

I have never been paid for the work. I do not know who or what is behind the people who ask me the questions—but they are connected to my organization somehow. I am doing the work of God, even when it's mysterious to me. I do not know what they do with the information.

It all began so simply. I was asked by a kind-looking man to see if I could find out the name of the new local police chief. He said he was a reporter and that he wanted to interview the chief. Everyone knew the former chief had been killed. The new one was keeping his head down. So I said sure, yes, and I did. Easy. No harm done, the pleasure of doing a stranger a simple favour. And then, a few weeks later, I was asked for some information again—this time by another man.

The second man began, by way of introduction, saying that the reporter was a friend of his, and that I'd been recommended by him as an excellent source of information. Flattered, I obliged. This became a pattern until soon the people who approached me needed no introduction.

For a time, I expected to be informed who precisely I was doing this for and when it might end. I thought one of these people asking for information might explain to me it was for this political party, or such and such a country's government, or else a media corporation, or activist organization. But nothing was ever forthcoming. I finally tried asking directly, and the person just smiled. Before turning to go, she said, Helen you are only ever working for God.

This work has become entangled in what I do, a part of who I am and how I conduct myself. I enjoy it. I have been chosen. I do not expect I'll ever know why. It takes courage to maintain this level of faith. And, the added danger it brings helps keep the pain away.

More shots, semi-automatic. The army is patrolling the streets. The faint cries of a woman—likely being dragged right out of her dreams—drift up into the night. Car horns are pressed as some choose to flee, fight to get out, get away. A man shouts. He is trying to attract attention as a call for help, or to scare assailants off. I smell burning rubber in the air.

About twenty-four hours ago I was asked by a tall woman in the downstairs lobby to approach the leather vendor across the road. Buy a suede bookmark, she said. When you do, he will tell you a day and perhaps also a time. I will be in the café. Come directly to me but do not let him see us speaking to one another. Ignore me if he follows you or if he can see us.

This request was different. I have never been asked to speak to someone and pass along messages, only to use my wits and try to casually find out simple facts. The leather vendor was there. I followed the woman's instructions.

Do you have a suede bookmark? I asked. He was a compact man with strong-looking arms.

You're a day late, he said. It will happen in five minutes, he added, handing me the bookmark, asking for no money in return. I took the bookmark and returned to the hotel's café. Paris was seated by the window. I joined him and ate some pastry. The woman entered and took the next table. Before she and I were able to speak, soldiers burst in. During the commotion, under her breath, she spoke to me. She was confused initially. I now understand it was because she was clearly annoyed at being caught up in the fall of the city. The information I was passing along was, obviously, the timing of the northern army's advance. So who is she? What business is she involved in? Peanut, I do not know. It is likely better I never find out.

The next few hours were harried. Even if my feelings for your father are only a fraction of those he has for me, I did not plan on being apart from him, on separating him from his baby daughter. Please know that this coup was unfolding around me and I did not know how to escape it.

They are going to take us too, she said. Stay close to me. I will tell you what to do.

Soldiers from the North invaded the city. They swarmed the Colonial Hotel and rounded up the foreigners, Paris and me included. We were loaded onto a large truck. A guard sat facing us at the front. He had a rifle of some sort. The woman assured me that she would see to it that I could leave, with her, and another woman. I asked her about Paris.

He's a doctor, I pleaded.

She said that the men would have to stay. But she would try to meet with the Colonel himself to see what she could do for Paris.

Who is this Colonel? I demanded.

The leather vendor you talked with, she said.

He can't just do this, I said. We are humanitarian aid workers.

She looked at me directly, and said straightforwardly that full-scale civil war had broken out. The government in the South is falling. We are inside chaos. There isn't an organization, or law, or government whose authority matters here. Stay close to me. I can get us back to the capital city—which has yet to fall and likely won't for weeks due to the distance over the mountains. From there, we'll see what can be bargained.

Peanut, I was scared—the machete blades, the cruelty of the soldiers. The road and dust made the journey difficult. Nausea came in waves. It seemed to me that this was a mistake, a detour that would be corrected. And it was. But, only partially so. As soon as we arrived at their camp in the mountains, the three women in the group—this woman, myself, and one other who had been muttering a prayer in French, were led to a jeep. As I climbed into the back seat I turned to look for Paris. To show him that I was alive and was being saved, to leave him with an impression of my face that said: *never lose hope*. But a large soldier was standing between us, blocking our line of sight. We pulled away with a jerk, the dust and engine noise and confusion taking a few moments to subside, and by that time we were beyond the camp.

Not far down the mountain, our jeep pulled aside to allow another to pass. The Colonel was in the passenger seat. He caught our eyes. Both jeeps stopped. He got out. The woman did too, approaching him. They spoke. She towered over him. When she returned to our jeep she said to me that she had struck a deal. Paris would be spared, she said. The Colonel would ransom him.

The best I could do, she said.

I am grateful.

Is he brave?

He isn't a coward.

Is he a reckless man?

I don't know, I said. I really don't know.

The jeep dropped us off at the Colonial Hotel where we found no one working, but it was intact. The phone line was dead. It was then that we came upon the food and water and locked ourselves in rooms upstairs. The woman said she would be gone at first light, but would be back for us within a matter of hours. What is your name? I asked her. She smiled and turned away.

=

Paris

AS THE TRUCK STOPPED, HELEN leaned into me. Up close to my face she said, Listen to me. When we get out I will be taken away. You must let me go. Don't put up a fight or they will kill you, Paris. Stay, just stay. You will be spared. They know you are a doctor; they need your help. And then she kissed me on the cheek, touching my face and the nape of my neck.

I did not properly comprehend all of what she was telling me. But I believed her. I always believed.

I grazed my knee stumbling off the truck. There was sudden, superficial blood and those about me offered the doctor help, in case, perhaps, it would oblige me to repay the favour when they needed it. Helen was next to me, but her focus was not my cut knee. Soldiers pressed us up against a mud wall.

One soldier with a pockmarked face brandished a machete as he strode the length of our line. Another followed him and tied a blindfold on each of us. Sharp bits of straw embedded in the mud wall pricked into my neck and head.

Where do you think we are? I asked Helen in a whisper. My other four senses were alive, eagerly seeking information. She did not answer. This air is thinner, I continued. Are we in the northern mountains? The truck had seemed to work its way up and down hills, but where and how many I couldn't say. The mountains to the north were the edge of these people's ancestral land. It would be known and safer ground for them.

Then I heard the sound of a gunshot, its imprecise ricochet, followed by struggling. I tilted my head toward the noise. My blindfold was not tied on well; I was able to see some of what was going on. At the end of the line, an execution, and then in poor English a soldier shouted threats.

You will be killed all! Do not run away! See this man? He runs. Will you run now?

The previous year—another country on another continent, another set of grim problems—we were all arrested and thrown into a football stadium to await our fate. But a production crew arrived making a documentary. They were shown where to come by several foreign aid workers that we knew. Caught on film, our captors ran away. The aid workers asked if we were hurt. The film's director instead asked how the situation made us feel as he pointed at us the very camera that had saved us.

The light was sudden and difficult. I was correct; we were up in the mountains. My blindfold had been ripped off. Why was it put on in the first place?

Along with two other foreign women—the woman from the café and the other one who had been praying in French—Helen was led over to a jeep. A soldier got in with them and removed their blindfolds. Then the soldier nearest me signalled to him, making a thrusting gesture with his pelvis. It was acknowledged by the soldier with a closed fist. I saw that Helen was disorientated. She attempted a look back at me, but was blocked by the body of the other soldier. I could see that she did not know where I was in relation to her. The jeep drove down and away. It must have appeared to her that I was following her instructions, obedient, acquiescing to the end—I did not run after her. But I wanted to. She was disappearing and my whole living being cried for her, desired her, would have gladly taken death as a preferred option over letting her leave me, but I was unable to talk, too frozen with horror to even cry out her name. I was struck silent, immobile and weak. Do you think less of me?

Daughter, I have no one to blame but myself. Despite the hopes and fears of the naive many, you can learn to love this lawless, Godless world. I have. I have come to understand my paralysis as an unwillingness to face my suspicions of her. I wanted Helen more than I wanted the truth of what she knew and who she really was. So I surrendered to her, gave you up, and was cast out into this abyss.

A thin dog was sniffing about and licked at my bloody leg. I attempted to push it off with my foot. The soldier approached me and booted the dog. The man was young and strong. He smiled at the sound of the dog's yelp. He walked over to it and stomped repeatedly on its head and neck until it ceased its cries, until it was dead. He then got close to my face, grimaced, and cocked his neck, preparing to head butt me. I winced, awaiting pain. Instead he laughed at my obvious fear. Called me *blind*.

At the end of the line a man raced through the Lord's Prayer in English—taking, I guess, his cue from the recently departed French woman. The soldiers understood him to be praying. After exchanging looks they shrugged, allowed him to continue. *Thy kingdom come; thy will be done*—his words found a new rhythm. It was the right time for these words; I was grateful to him, for the lulling, and I relaxed by accepting in the straw points from the wall needling my neck, and breathed into and through the pain of it. Helen was taken from me. My daughter, what of you, still an embryo deep in her womb, did you survive this day?

A white jeep pulled up, driven by a short man wearing fatigues. I did not immediately see his face. He was carrying a handgun—*as we forgive them that trespass against us.*

Are you from the oil company or the bank? the soldier demanded of a bald man just three people away from me. There was a fresh and serious savageness to this soldier's voice—I did not risk looking up again. *And lead us not into temptation; but deliver us from evil.*

I am from the bank, said the man. In his voice there was gratitude, hope. I understood that he believed that this soldier had come to release him: his global bank perhaps having paid some extortion fee to save their loyal employee. *For thine is the kingdom, the power, and the glory.* The soldier began to walk away, but turned and quickly unloaded four bullets into the man. The noise of it was horribly loud. I strained for breath and felt light-headed. Another person in line vomited. The bald man fought to stay upright but folded forward facedown onto the ground. Blood pooled from him. The shooter was the leather vendor I had seen across the street from the hotel.

Another soldier saluted him and called him Colonel. They embraced, the salute mere pretence or play between two old friends. Their garbled talk was light and familiar. I did not understand it, but I followed the tones. Did they talk of easy things? Were they catching up and gathering simple information, the weather up higher in the mountains or the cost of food on the black market in the capital, or perhaps the name of a trusted colleague working in the city in disguise?

They switched abruptly to English.

Lend me your gun, friend, said the Colonel.

I thought another, maybe several, among us would now be shot. But instead this man then called to the soldier who had kicked the dog away from me. The gun was thrown to him. Two hidden soldiers burst in from a tent behind a stand of trees, a camp that I had not previously taken in. There was shouting among them. The friend's gun had not been borrowed. The Colonel was not his trusted friend. The friend had been double-crossed, or tricked or suckered by the Colonel. The friend had terror on his face and he pleaded, as his own gun fired a bullet into his stomach.

The soldiers followed the orders given by the Colonel and the friend's body was thrown beside the dead banker. The Colonel shot the friend's corpse in the head one more time. He then stood over the body and I heard the sound, louder than one might expect, of his urine as it splashed into the pooled blood and dust about the bald man's head.

===

Helen

THE WOMAN KNOCKED LOUDLY ON the door of my room in the Colonial Hotel. It was mid morning. She woke me from an unintentional doze. I was surprised to see her return at all. I stuffed Paris's drugs, razor, and photograph album into my bag, leaving the rest of his belongings in the room. I realized that he must have had his passport and wallet with him. They'll take those at the first opportunity.

Outside, the woman urged me down a series of back alleys at a half run. The day was hot. Shots were ringing out frequently. Livestock was loose—chickens, goats, pigs. Fires burned. The flies were bad. At one intersection music boomed from a truck radio. Soldiers were ransacking a store. We pressed on unseen.

Where is the other one, the French woman? I asked.

She left, said the woman. I didn't ask anything more.

We entered a two-storey brown building that appeared to be a mechanic's garage. Inside was an old bus. It was full of women and children—and had been waiting for me. The engine turned over. The garage doors swung open to the street and the bus jolted forward into the daylight. Would we be allowed to leave the town? The woman did not get on the bus. She did not even say goodbye.

I sat next to a mother with a baby that had dysentery and an angry diaper rash that flowered down her legs and up onto her stomach. Neither the mother nor I had creams. I shared my water. There were chickens in cages tied to the roof of the bus and at the back a group of children periodically tried singing songs.

The driver's name was Oenone. She seemed to me at first glance another strong-looking local woman with closely cropped hair. She took the corners quickly and the bus pitched, struggling with the angles at such speed. Within a few minutes we were in the slums. The northern soldiers did not yet seem to be about—in this part of the town. Our driver pressed on just as fast. She shifted gears with much physical effort. Only when the open road began, and the town fell away behind us, did she moderate her pace. The tension inside the bus diminished.

After about two hours the bus stopped at a village. I'd been there before. It's the last place to refuel and rest at the edge of the plains before tackling the roads through the southern mountains. A crowd had gathered in the town's square. There were many who had fled and had reached this village before us. We stayed on the bus, opening the windows to let in air, to hear. The mother beside me spoke English well. She worked for the oil company, she told me.

Everyone on this bus has some connection to the company, she said. We are servants of employees and their families mostly. What is your connection to the company? Do you work for it?

I told her the truth. That I was a nurse from the camps, caught up in the town when the soldiers arrived.

The crowd was becoming agitated, arguments erupting. I asked her what they were saying. Her baby was fussing. She strained to hear.

They do not believe what is happening, she said. They are asking Oenone if they should continue on through the mountains in their cars or on their donkeys. What about those on bicycles or on foot? They are concerned they will not make it, and are questioning how bad things back in the town really are.

After a time Oenone got off the bus and addressed the crowd. She was animated and used her muscular arms as she talked. At first I didn't need a translation. She spoke slowly and through gesture and the few words I knew, she made clear that everyone should continue on to the capital. Oenone carried gravity and seemed used to being in front of crowds. Then she sped up her speech.

What now? I asked the mother.

She is saying that no matter how long it takes, we must all go. Nowhere on this side of the mountains will be safe before long. But it's our home, some in the crowd are pleading. The soldiers will return to the North after they take what they need from us! But Oenone says, No, they will not leave. They will stay.

Next a man spoke for some time. Don't believe her, he said. Our government will soon be here to push them back. He said more, but the woman was unable to hear.

Oenone remained commanding. She was not a bus driver I understood, but a leader of some sort. The crowd knew her. They listened when she climbed up on a fruit cart and demanded silence.

She is saying that our town and the entire plains region have fallen into the hands of the northerners. She is saying that everyone must flee. We are at war.

Then I heard Oenone, with raw emotion in her voice, use the word for *them*.

A man then pointed at her and spoke accusingly.

What, what? I asked the woman.

He says that her husband is behind all this.

Oenone then shook her head. She said that the Colonel is no longer her husband. He is a northern traitor. She then climbed aboard the bus and started it up. We sprang forward and before long were making our way up the first gentle incline of the foothills.

When the woman's baby settled down I asked about the driver. She's the government official for the city, said the woman. Oenone is a healer. An organizer of opinions. She has one child. Her former husband was the government official before her, but he broke her heart when he sided with the northerners whose army was becoming ever more powerful with money from the oil company. When she found out about his dealings, she ran him out of town. It was Oenone who the people really loved all along.

Where is he now?

He is the leader of the northern army. They are our enemies. This was his bus, said the woman. He used to fix everyone's cars and he ran the only buses across the plains to and from the town. Then he ran for government leader of the plains region. She was the reason he won. He said *No corruption*! But all the time the oil company paid him with money and fuel for his buses. They are powerful. Then Oenone found out that her husband was taking oil company money. She stood before the town and told everyone. They made her the leader. Her husband escaped into the night. But it is said that before he did, he held her down one last time, leaving her with his seed. She carried the baby inside her proudly anyway. This is my baby, she said. Not his. Oenone is the mother of our town. We are all her children.

The woman shared her lunch with me. I gave her some money. For your baby, I said when she tried to refuse. At the front of the bus, Oenone pressed on and on.

Peanut, my own mother gave me my name, and then gave me up. Or, if I could hear her tell it, would she say that she gave me a name and then was not allowed to give me anything more? I am part indigenous. If you know the look, you can see the history in my face. Many back home do. They are forced to see it even when they are not looking for it. I notice a quiver come over them, a goose crossing their grave, or their ancestor's grave, perhaps.

Ours is a bloody and shame-riddled history too. Which country's isn't?

Confronted with my face, even if I am happy and smiling, the fact of it implies agony. Mine is a face of loss. So they are sorry and sometimes they ask outright after my story, and other times they weakly mind their own business. In my face, my skin, my body, they take in the full Pyrrhic victory. I am stolen land, erased language, an echo of rapes long ago. And the men especially continue to stare, taking in my looks, which I understand to be beautiful. Some can't shake me. I become an idea of myself, of Helen, and I haunt them, poison their dreams. At first they think it's love, of the mad, obsessive kind. But these are simply the aftershocks of our joint violence. It's not love they feel, but the burn of disgrace.

When Paris sees me it's different. His love is free of politics. Which is shallow, I suppose. But it's also love that is particular, just for me. The ghosts cannot find our bed.

I grew up in foster homes and, near the end, in a group house run by an agency. I lived under the care of kind women and drunken men, or drunken women and kind men. My faith was my companion, my consolation. Before I began nursing for the organization, I'd rented a ground floor flat on the esplanade. It was not far from the happiest place I'd lived during my whole childhood. While I lived there, I often visited Mum. The only woman I ever named as such. It was my choice to call her Mum. And I still do. She kept me with her as long as she was able. Then she needed to care for her husband fulltime. They were old—too old to be my parents then. She's eighty now. I miss her tonight as I write this. I pray you'll meet her someday.

The flat I lived in had yellow brick. Neighbours looked after one another. I got up early in the mornings. I'd be just sitting and looking out, taking in the horizon. I worked at the hospital, many night shifts. One neighbour in particular would see me there and often pop round with a cup of tea, or call out a bright *good morning* to me. This is how I went on. It was all so beautiful and so painful, too silent and too safe. I knew I had to go. I looked out at that horizon, thinking of what lay beyond it, and how I could get there. How I could get rid of this aching pain I had deep inside me.

Peanut, this is your mother speaking. I was given up—and I don't know why. What kind of mother will I be? How will I know what to do? I don't mean the simple things, like feed, clothe, and shelter. I mean the deeper attachments. How do they begin? Do you trigger them, or do I? If it's me, if that's my job, will I? Can I? What if I'm no different than her, my biological mother? What if I see you and hand you away, simply saying, No. No, this is not mine, I do not want her, I didn't mean for her to come, take her away. What if this kind of cruelty runs deep, or is God's will. What if it can't be helped?

=====

Paris

MY DAUGHTER, I CONFESS, I can feel your presence. I have always believed that you were born and that you do live. But what about Helen, is she alive too? Did she tell you my name? Do you ever look into your own eyes and wonder if they are your father's? Do our ears make a similar shape? Do you have a cowlick that goes like mine?

I have lived an incarcerated life, removed from the world and burdened with so much deadly time. I have held you, in my mind, at every age. I have imagined soothing your infant cry. I cared for you when you were teething and feverish. I caught you as you took those first steps. As a young girl I helped you learn to ride your bike and together we baked cookies. When you became so cross and announced that you intended to run away, I walked to the corner with you and helped you cross the road—and yes I scooped you up, wiped your tears away, and carried you home.

I have had so much time.

All those fatherly duties and joys, and a thousand others I have invented for us. We know one another as if it had all occurred, just as it should have.

There is one matter though that I cannot decide upon. One agony that has resided in my heart because, despite having tried, it is a fact I cannot allow myself to err on, much less invent. If you would, sweet daughter of mine, please, tell me your name?

Along with a half dozen other men I was walked in a line through dense bush, a soldier at each end. The track was narrow and muddy. I wore brogues and still had on my white and green shirt. After an hour we came upon a large clearing in the forest that overlooked a valley. The clearing housed a recently built prison compound. An established local village with mud-walled houses and several larger community buildings was farther down the hill. There was a sign for Pepsi-Cola, and a sleeping goat tied to a post. It was dusk.

Once inside, for a time we were tied to a fence, our hands lashed behind our backs, the rope knotted through the wire. A cool mist ebbed down the mountain. In the courtyard of the compound, huddling together, fifty men pressed against one another, against the damp. The night sky, now filled with stars and a half moon, blinked between rolls of barbed wire. We were untied and walked into the compound proper. A generator motored on. The electrified fence hummed. We stayed together, sitting in a similar fashion to the others, in a closed group. Improbably, I slept.

As dawn came, inky and hesitant, the guards encircled the yard, carrying three naked flame torches that gave unstable light. Some held guns, their faces grinning and righteous. They were boys—no more than twelve—obviously new recruits. How different was this than a child's game to them? They were swollen with confidence and it seemed effortless and magical that they had traded poverty and boyhood for instant manhood and power. Several others, those carrying the torches, were more reserved, older, serious, and in charge.

We were untied and instructed to lie on the ground, clasp our hands together in front of us. Our faces were flush against the dirt and many men with whom I lay whimpered and shivered as I did. Some of those captured in the compound were police, still in uniform, from the South.

Three police patrolling the petrol station by the river

have not responded to radio contact since Tuesday. They are
presumed captured, or killed, during recent skirmishes with
soldiers from the North, say government sources.

Why, as I read the report that morning, did I not imagine that a compound such as this could be their fate?

Some frenzied shouts and whoops erupted from just beyond the electric fence. The early morning smelled first of fuel and then of burning flesh.

It reminded me of a burn victim I'd once treated in the hospital's emergency room back home. A different tragedy, a lifetime ago. We'd air lifted him to a specialized burn unit in another city.

Then the early sky was brightened by a pyre of bodies, a chorus of mouths aghast in disbelief, a crowd of faces cinched and lips stricken, a congregation of arms stiff with their fingers rigid pointing upward—at what, God? We could do nothing but look on as the burn of humans and kerosene went shushing out into the open, wet morning. Is everything as it was elsewhere, I wondered; was I still among the living?

For days we were held in that yard. Those closest to the kitchen window caught and repeated sentences, mouth to ear, eagerly snatched from the cook's gossip. All news was interpreted, and reinterpreted, however banal. Our bodies craved information as much as calories. During the day we smelled the onions being cut and cooked. Hot orange water from boiled root vegetables was thrown out the back door of the kitchen and it washed through the compound. They handed out cups of food twice a day.

In the beginning, the end had seemed certain. That in a matter of hours we would be lined up and shot, that we too would be burned as a group. Yet, as one day came and went, from the cook's gossip, from the loose lips of one of the guards, we learned that instead we would be made to work. A new jail was to be built. The captured police would be enslaved. The dozen or so blind would be kept too, held for ransom, when the conditions were right.

My daughter, let me go back. I was not without my mind. Helen and I became one, the way lovers do. Drawn together easily enough. She chased war zones and hot spots, the taste and thrill, the adrenaline and fatigue of it, the righteousness and purposefulness of it all. Those were her reasons, I believe.

We could really use you, in an ongoing way, the organization's executive director had said to me on the phone at the conclusion of my first assignment.

It was supposed to have been a onetime mission, a learning and growth experience for me.

Helen and I met and worked together on that first mission. Her looks were impossible to ignore. I was self-conscious around her. But that was all. Did I know then? That I would develop such love for her? That I was even capable of such desire? My thought though was that I was returning home to my clean and safe apartment. I'd been away for three weeks.

I understand, the executive director pressed on, that you are a fine doctor, that you're making friends, and suit the work. What can I offer you to lure you back? I cannot pay more than the pittance I do, I'm sorry. Anyone in particular that you enjoyed working with, that you would choose, given the option, to be paired up with on reassignments?

I had been on a team working with three nurses. Helen was one of them. Was she implying I could choose the most attractive of them to work with? I turned the executive director down. Needing to make more money and restart real life, I returned home.

Helen wrote me an email. First, just the one. But we soon, and easily, began a correspondence. I remember some of what she wrote—the essence. Her voice in them is still clear to me.

Paris,

> *Yesterday I pulled out a tire iron lodged
> in a boy's leg. We were deep in a field.
> The screaming will stay with me for
> weeks. The girls say hello. Tomorrow
> we are all going to a movie. A movie!
> It won't be in English, but who cares, a
> story to take me away to some other place
> for a few hours.*

Yours, Helen

There would be none for weeks while she worked
on the front lines, then seven in three days as she
rested and needed to write and tell some of what
she'd experienced. They were always short but never
shied away from the horror and reality of the work
before her.

Paris,

> *Do you know much about Dengue
> Fever? We are seeing it a lot down
> here. We have not had a physician with
> us for this past week—neither Bill nor
> Donna is available. People presenting
> in such pain, high temps, the rash etc.*

We are all doing what we can to stay away from mosquitoes. Sleeping under nets. Burning local herbs even. I've never seen such poor drinking water. It looks like dishwater after curry. The locals all play instruments in the evenings and dance. They are very colourful. Not a penny among them, but stunning artists, determination, ingenuity, and much joy. They tear at my heart. God must love them.

Yours, H.

I wrote her long emails after my shift at the hospital, deep into the night. I would try to keep them light, telling of world news and pleasant touches that happened during my day. I began to think about her more often than not.

The executive director mailed me a photograph of Helen with some of the other nurses on the team. They had been taken as a part of a professional photo shoot that the organization was using to fundraise. On the surface it operated similar to all the NGOs. At its roots, however, it was a splintered-off faction of a fundamentalist Christian organization. I had struggled with that aspect—assumed that its mission was to first save the life, then save the soul.

But they never proselytized on the front lines. They said grace at mealtimes, and some would offer short prayers at the bedside of a dying patient, but the conversation among the nurses was as frank as I'd come to expect anywhere. I was left to my agnostic and scientifically minded self.

An idea grew in me. I kept thinking about it, about her. I did miss the thrilling importance of the work; I ached to be nearer to Helen. I contacted the executive director.

Changed my mind, I said.

I guessed right about you, she said. Bless you.

May I tell you, my daughter, of how Helen and I finally came together? Is it awkward? Some children do not want to hear of these moments. If you are like me, you will always be hungrier for more information, and that will smother any schoolgirl embarrassment.

Helen and I became one through exhaustion. We had connected while we worked with a group of children at a bombed-out church. We taught them math for an afternoon and created a false world of normalcy in the middle of their horror. See, we tried to say, even at the world's end, there is school, there is boredom, there is free time and space to play in a yard. We took this small gesture on together without thought as a task ordered by no one and overseen only by ourselves or, for Helen, perhaps by God. Instead of looking in vain for their parents buried in rubble, the children came and practised addition, subtraction. Something about this day, or perhaps it was an accumulation of days, drew us closer together.

We needed to escape, a break. I urged Helen to come with me—although I would not have left without her—and she agreed. We took a long truck ride across a guarded border, then a passenger train. Finally, we emerged as two educated, privileged adults, showered and preened, in a room at a Hilton. We were safe. We lay down together.

I saw the last raw strands of sun leave her body as it set behind that exhausted, naked continent we were on. Later, after some sleep, but still during the night, Helen spoke. Can I do this? she asked as she climbed onto me, easing her body down, more slowly than was necessary. The scars and bruises on her body from the work, the stars through the window in the dark, these gave me the strength to see that this service and my life was bigger than I was.

Looking up, as if to heaven, she said, I should not be afraid. I know why I am doing this.

I saw the sun rise over her the next morning, glinting off the city towers, chrome, glass, altering all of my aspects, thoughts, and perspectives. I was taken. I saw a river. I travelled on boats using winds on a reach for the mouth. I saw ruins. I guessed at the history. I fell effortlessly in love.

Can I do this? she asked again and again.

Yes, I said. We can, we can.

By the time we checked out I knew that I would never be going home—that, like her, I had none. We would be each other's home.

My daughter, does she remember this as I do? We stole the robes and slippers from the room, gave them to a woman begging in the street. Is this how she weaves it or have the details been altered or embroidered with time and retelling? Take these, we said to the beggar and we laughed the giddy laughter of two people who had changed their minds about what could and could not be done and together were charging ahead to someplace wondrous and unknown.

Helen

IT IS NIGHT AND WE have stopped. We have passed through the foothills and the large mountains are before us. Oenone tells us that the bus does not have working headlights and the roads ahead are steep and difficult. We will set off again at sunrise. The air is cool and the sky is lighter than usual because of a full, white moon. Some of the women stayed on the bus. Others, myself included, got off and stretched out on the ground, resting on a piece of clothing or luggage. The earth is weathered and old-looking here. I was alone for some time, left to listen to the murmurs of mothers calming their babies. For some moments there was only sleeping. The sounds of the cooling bus engine clicked into the evening. I can see well enough to write if I angle my page skyward at the moon.

Then Oenone came to me. She was carrying

a torch, fire burning on the end of a twist of thick reeds. Her face flickered.

You are a foreign nurse? The herbs are not working, she said hurriedly. My child is dying. His face is telling me he is dying.

I recognized the controlled distress of a mother. From my backpack I grabbed my stethoscope and the small first aid kit that I carry. I was brought to her son, a boy of about four or five whom I'd seen sitting up on the bus seat behind her, smiling, only hours before. Now he was lying on dry grass a short walk away from the bus at the edge of some bush. Oenone had a wet cloth on his forehead. I peeled it away. She had put some herb or leaf under the cloth, and the child seemed to have some in his mouth which I saw as he began to cough and vomit.

This boy was very sick. His pulse was rapid. He then began to have difficulty breathing. I listened to his chest, an erratic heartbeat. Oenone was crying something in her language over and over again, then she began making a sound and waving her arm, first in the air, then along the ground, and just as I realized that she was telling me the boy had been bitten by a snake, I came upon the puncture wound. It was on his left calf. The hugely swollen leg. His pulse thinned. Then his respiratory function collapsed. He arrested. A small body that had no chance. I worked on him for several more minutes but was never able to retrieve him.

I looked up as I stopped. Oenone's face opened and I felt, rather than heard, the sound that came from her—a hoarse, angry, terrified scream of disbelief, of self blame, of rage that reached into the mountains, bouncing back and forth with menacing accusation. She scooped up the boy's body and ran a distance with it until she fell to her knees to begin a keening that is still continuing as I write this now. Other women on the bus have gone to be with her, joining with her, in a rhythmical way that would have an element of song, were it not so painful. They cry and wail, the way blood pumps, the way the days come and go, the way a tide washes in and away.

Peanut, I have this in store? The risk of enduring such total loss? I would sooner choose myself. I must go to be with her, if I'm allowed.

Oenone's mourning cries continued all night. When I went to her, one woman stood to leave as I joined, and the others remained. I followed along, taking two handfuls of dirt, breathing in as they did, allowing the sorrow to come out of me, the completeness of it rushing upward and out, in violent throbs. I cried with them, yes for Oenone's boy, but also for myself, until I had nothing left but a connection to the earth and God. I left them and slept until the first light came over the mountaintops, finding us down here in these cool foothills.

Oenone came to me in the morning. She had a calm about her. She did not look tired, or bereft, but instead she reached out her fingers and touched my cheek. She thanked me for trying to save her boy.

I knew I waited for you to get on the bus for a reason, she said.

I apologized for not being able to save him. But she stopped me. She said I'd been on the bus to show that *nothing* could have saved him. Not local cures, not foreign medicine. Without me, she might have always wondered.

Some of the women and their young boys were gathering wood, dragging dead branches into a pile, gathering long grass. It was lit with a petrol swoosh. The bus was now empty of passengers. We stood gathered around the large fire. Oenone brought her son's body to the edge of it. She then looked away.

Another woman used a rock to strike the boy's mouth and reached into it, bringing out a front tooth. The woman handed it to Oenone, who clamped both her hands around it.

The child was then doused in petrol and

thrown onto the fire. The crowd of us stood for a moment to witness the engulfing.

We boarded the bus, tired, shaken. With Oenone still at the wheel, we began a slow and difficult trip through the southern mountains bound for the capital city.

My daughter, I looked back through the open window as we drove away. I suspect that I was alone in this. For some reason, I needed to see the scene without people. By the side of the road I saw a boy's small body being cremated. The pyre was already burning down, his body lost within it, taken by the smoke, and the flames, and the sparks.

The sun now streamed through the pass in the mountains ahead, lighting up the plain that extended on to the horizon. I have seen so much death. But it's really only the dying that I see. The clinical last few days or moments. I do not attend the funerals. I do not weep with the widows or orphans, with the parents, with the community. I write facts on a sheet, seek a doctor's signature for a chart.

The smoke trails upward, the wind taking Oenone's son into the air, into itself. With each breath, peanut, you and I become nearer to death, taking the dead into our lungs. But with you inside me, I bring you toward life.

I have chosen you. For now, you are in me. When I have you, then you will be only you. And you too will breathe this world's air, with its agony, its mountain pass beauty and life.

I do not have her inner strength. Oenone carries the ferociousness of motherhood into her every purpose. She drives, she acts, she consoles others, all with it. Where does this power come from? Can I learn? Can I become so invested in others that I no longer see myself as having an end? This is how she is. She carries a force with her, a burden that she does not question, but rather accepts and uses. She takes on this weight that others would simply fall under, and instead makes it hers, showing us all how to work with it and not against it.

Oenone adds to the world. I subtract from it.

Next to her, even though I am a nurse, I am delicate and pretty. My life, one that I considered unfairly difficult and something to escape from, I see now as vain and trivial. I deserve no pity. Peanut, with you though, I will begin to add. I will try to be like her. I promise. I will ask God for this.

The bus made the journey slowly although the roads were clear of soldiers. When we arrived, Oenone parked at the sea wall off the main square of the downtown. There was traffic—trucks and buses, cars and bicycles that had travelled from all across the country. We disembarked and most of the women and children gathered beside the bus on some grass and awaited Oenone's next instructions.

I looked into Oenone's face, searching, I think, for any final words, directions for how I should act in this world. She smiled.

Goodbye my *blind* sister, she said. I wish you happiness and good health for the baby you carry. And as she said those words I saw, finally, that she looked tired.

Get some sleep soon, I said.

This is not my sea. It is not, but the salt and wind of this place is enough. This afternoon I stood on the top of a hill overlooking the shallow harbour where the capital sits like a bird's nest. I felt a pull toward home. It was the seagulls. What is it about seagulls that make them native to everywhere? I see them wherever I go. Even in countries that are inland with vast lakes, not oceans, seagulls bob and float about, squawking. Like me, these birds make every place home.

The sea is easy to read if you know it well enough. If the lost hours of your childhood were spent sitting in front of the sea, watching the wind on it, the weather forecast itself with whitecaps and clouds, with seaweed, the surface schools of fish shimmering in explosive escape, and treacly crimson and ginger sunsets. Then wherever you go, you can read the sea.

Will you be able to?

I'd never thought about that before today. Standing there on that hill, taking in the subtle shifts of wind and current, I sensed a change was on its way, a storm. If this was my home then I would know what kind of wind it was, what it had in store—such as the southerly wind that carries cool air, or a dark squalling nor'easter with storm and rain, or else a hot westerly with its dry and awful relentlessness.

Here I could not tell exactly what was to come. This is not my sea. But I knew the beginnings of movement on the sea. I know how to read change on the ocean because it's a part of who I am. And, peanut, as my hand rested across my stomach instinctively, I wondered if you will also learn to read change on the sea.

You will, if I choose it for you.

At the bottom of the hill two boys were fishing with short lines rolled up around pieces of wood. They were tossing their lines into the water near the rock pools where the last licks of water were ebbing with the gentle current. From time to time one of them would reel in a thin, silvery fish. Without talking he would grasp it in one hand, take out the hook, and toss it into a metal container behind him. There was almost no talk between the boys. Perhaps they were brothers; they looked alike and one was taller than the other. A stray dog looking for food or attention trotted past and stuck its nose into the container. One of the boys turned and stamped his foot; the dog continued on its way.

Many of the houses along the coast have white walls with pitched terracotta roofs or shiny metal flat ones and either green or blue painted front doors. Palm trees and other low shrubs lined the shore. People came and went easily, as if there were no war happening on the other side of the mountains, the range giving them immunity. The mountains themselves then drifted off into the background haze as I turned and looked inland. This was the direction from where I'd come on the bus.

Along the short beach at the end of the harbour was a market where merchants sold fruit and carpets, donkeys and tires for trucks and cars. I'd wandered through it before deciding to walk up the hill. The market had an atmosphere to it that I had grown used to, an air that everything was negotiable. I bought a bowl of noodles and meat, which I ate with a plastic fork before walking farther and farther up the hill. Plastic forks—some evidence the world was still functioning properly here, I thought.

I hadn't planned on getting all the way to the top of the hill, but was glad I did once I'd arrived and sat to rest. How right and elemental it all felt.

The boys fishing, the clouds, sensing the change on the ocean made me feel in control.

One of the boys caught a squid. The other became animated. This was clearly an unexpected catch. Perhaps it meant money. In any case, the lines were wound in and the metal bucket was filled with enough water to keep the catch fresh. The boys made their way back along the path below me toward the market and the port. I looked back the other way for the dog, to see if it was lurking.

I was about to stand and make my way down when I spotted a figure walking up the hill toward me. It was a nursing colleague—a newer girl I didn't know well. I waved as she came closer and she did the same in return.

I saw you at the market, she said. I tried to catch up, but I lost you. I was about to turn back when I looked up, and there you were, on top of this hill.

She and the others who had been at the camp were driven in a convoy back to the capital as word of the growing coup reached them. They had been stranded here for three days, awaiting instructions on how they were to get out. She told me that while they knew Paris and I had been on leave in the town, they were unable to take that route due to the insurgency. They had expected to see us here, already in the capital.

We were jealous of you, she said. You must

have gotten out so easily compared to us—still in the camp. Then she asked after Paris. I was not ready to answer her. I did not want to worry her. Perhaps I was concerned how she might take the news, or what she might do with the information.

He's alive, I said, waving my arm in a general sweep at the sprawling city and the mountains beyond, suggesting vaguely, he's there somewhere. She did not press further.

We talked then about the work, the organization, gossiped about others with whom we nursed. I believe she was looking to strike an alliance. She likely sensed in me a colleague who might help her see through the complicated parts of this work, the politics and the personal conflicts. Normally, I took in stray birds. This time though I stayed detached. I felt unwilling to commit to her. Like this strange sea, I was undergoing change. Committing to something else, someone else would have been in bad faith. So I remained kind, but guarded. She sensed my reserve and respected it. We returned together down the hill, not cementing a secret pact, but commenting on the sea, the difficult life that awaited the people here. I felt in her something of myself when I began this job—an eagerness to impress, to be in the thick of the action. It was her turn.

I reached the executive director on one of the few telephones still connected in the city. We talked only briefly, her responses and questions colliding into my own words echoing back at me in a frustrating delay that allowed no conversational rhythm to develop. She did, however, grasp what I was telling her. She knew how serious the matter was and I was reassured by her use of the phrases *report to the government*, and *friend of one of the board members will know what action to take*. The executive director instructed me to get on the first plane I could and remain with the others. She assured me they were praying for our safe return.

But I did not want to be with the others at all. They were suffocating me. I wanted to be free from their grip. If I went to them, the questions would mount quickly and I would not be able to deflect them as easily as I had done with the new girl. Eventually, questions of paternity and my physical and mental state would surface through insinuation. My professional capability would be called into question not directly, but through inference or omission.

They wouldn't understand. This is all for you. All because of you, peanut. There had been no other option for me there on that mountainside than to follow instructions, no explaining the woman who sought the information from the leather vendor.

None of the real story would be admissible. And I have no ability to invent plausible, alternative stories either.

So I made the decision to hide out and wait here for Paris, and then escape with both of you. I will not get on the same plane as the other nurses. Instead, I'll lie low another few days and wait. He will come. He must. We'll use this moment to leave the organization altogether. Despite the obvious danger to me and you, peanut, the way out of my life as I knew it is before me. We can leave the secrets and horrors behind. We have Paris now.

My peanut, deep inside me, you are changing me with every decision I make. I didn't meet the new girl and the others at the expensive hotel on the corner of the main boulevard as I'd said. Instead, I went back to Oenone's bus. I waited for her until the sun set for the evening. She did not return. Unsure of where to go or what to do, I wandered in the opposite direction from that hotel and my nursing colleagues.

The streets were clearing as the night air rolled down from the mountains. A narrow hotel that had signs in English came into view. Running out of choices I checked in. The porter behind the desk gave me a brass key and I bought two tins of Fanta from him. Off the lobby to one side was a small bar. It had a pool table. About a dozen local men were drinking beer. They were watching a game of soccer on a television.

My room, though clean, had no electric light, a single bed, and no sheets. There was just a mattress on a metal frame with slats underneath. The window looked onto the street below. I stood at it for a while, taking in the darkening sky. The smell of the sea was in the air. I heard the sounds of a far-off car horn and, closer, the hostile laughter of drinking men. I would not be able to eat this evening—it would be too dangerous to go out after dark. I used my backpack, which I had been carrying all day, as a pillow. I ate a mango and a tin of sardines, what I'd managed to carry in my pack from the Colonial Hotel. While it felt good to stretch across the bed, sleep did not come. I grew anxious. So, I am writing this down, for you, in case.

Later in the night, with almost no light to see, I began a letter. In case I am killed before Paris comes to me and neither of us get out of this country, I wrote to the executive director. Reiterating, expanding upon, our incomplete telephone conversation, I left my letter with the hotel porter the next morning. I asked him to mail it the minute the postal services were again working. He took my money for a stamp, some extra for his trouble. I held his eye. My attempt to reinforce his obligation having accepted my money. A message in a bottle might be more effective. I felt I had to do everything I could to ensure someone knew the threads of information I had about Paris. Or else I had to relieve myself of a burden. The weight of being the sole custodian of the facts.

I've stayed in the hotel for three nights. Despite my continual sense of danger, I was not prepared to risk confronting my colleagues. It was an unsafe decision, I know. But it was how I felt. Sometimes the right thing to do also means chancing it against longer odds.

During the days I can wander the city streets because people are about. The capital is not under siege but southern soldiers, loyal to the government, are at the corners. They carry automatic weapons. These men, some still with a bit of childhood lingering about their faces, hand out stern looks to most. As I pass, their eyes run the length of my body. One sucks air between his teeth, as if the sight of me causes his groin unjust pain. Today, an older soldier stepped in my way. He reached out with a finger, slowly, pressing it into my throat.

Please, I say.

I have money, he says.

I step away and hurry off, not looking back. It's only broad daylight and the great throngs of people going about their business in the city that fend him off.

I normally don't read newspapers. That was something Paris loved to do. He read them out to me. Badger me until I would listen, or comment, on this headline or that. But I spotted an edition in English one afternoon. I read it eagerly. The news gave nothing of the town we'd been captured in. Nothing of Paris, a captured *blind doctor*. Just stories with place names I did not know and leaders I did not recognize. That is, until I was turning the last page and there before me was a photograph of the Colonel. He was in full uniform—the picture did not appear to be recent.

Kind, sweet Paris, I miss you. I kept the newspaper. All of it, pushing all evidence of it down into my backpack.

On my walks, I also look for Oenone, even ask strangers if they know her, or have seen her. Her bus is no longer parked where it had been. None of the nearby merchants know of her, or recall her taking the bus.

I was able to find the mother who'd been my seat partner for the bus ride. She had mentioned that her sister lived in the capital next to a huge church. I recalled this when such a church happened to be right in front of me at the end of a wide avenue. I knocked on the door of the house beside it, trying my luck. There she was, sitting with her baby at a table in the middle of the room. She was pleased to see me. I ate with them that evening and they accepted nothing from me in return. I was their *honoured* guest. I refused the hoppy beer, my peanut, thinking of your growing body and brain. I explained to them why I would not accept it but they didn't understand my reasoning at all. It sounded awkward even to me, given the dangers all around me. Before nightfall I rose to leave. I needed to make the walk in the light. My friend understood and touched my stomach, spoke a few words in her language, and smiled. I kissed her baby, the smell of sour milk in the folds of its neck, its fragile skin. Soon, soon.

The blast hit me in a wave of force and glass and grit. I do not remember falling or landing, just shielding my eyes and face on the ground. From the shops people staggered, as if drunk, covered in white plaster dust, ruby-coloured blood soaking their clothes. The silence of the after moments was lingering. Then pain. Then screaming. The agony of opened up stomachs, torn limbs, lost faces. I staggered through it. A burning car. A child. Yellow lentils underfoot. A dead donkey, flies already at it. Unhurt people screaming, pointing, names and words and instructions and demands. The dead thrown over shoulders. Wailing women. Searching, calling out. Bells, church bells. Men with machine guns on a flatbed truck.

My hand is trembling. I found my way to the hotel room. The kindness of a stranger. I write knowing I can wait no longer. Peanut, you must survive. We must leave now. So this is what I do—I gather my belongings. I clutch my money. First I go across the park and down to the seashore. The pebbles under my feet. I splash the saltwater onto my face. Wash the blood and dust from my hands and arms. I am not hurt. I am hungry. I am thirsty. I am tired. I go to the expensive hotel and find a taxi driver. He takes me to the airport. I meet a man with a plane. I give him some money and board his single engine plane.

Once in the clouds the world below gave way, the hum and throttle of it sending me off to sleep. We landed several hours later in the neighbouring country, a place with a long-standing government and an operating international airport.

I lined up to purchase a ticket on the only international flight out that day. I didn't understand the language being spoken around me. I ate a plate of meat and rice.

As the plane left the tarmac that evening and the cabin announcements began in English, I exhaled deeply. The steward's rote performance reciting the safety regulations script was the relaxing signal for which my body was waiting.

Peanut, we made it. I have chosen you above all else. Will Paris forgive me for leaving him behind? Can women control when, and why, men are taken by war? It's a wound inflicted upon us again and again. To heal, we must let go. I see now that I am like Oenone. I too will become stronger. I have faith. From here on, it's you and me.

PART TWO: PARIS

Who will forget Helen? Not Paris, feverish, with the wild
eyes of Oenone watching his death.

—H.D., *Helen in Egypt*

Paris

THEY HAD WALKED IN, PURPOSEFULLY placing six knives in the dust of the compound. I was among two dozen or so men. We all stood back until they left.

This is a test, said someone.

We are watched, said another. The knives are not to be touched. This was what we all agreed. For the rest of the afternoon we walked around them. Always eyeing them slant, leaving them unreferenced in whatever conversations we had. The first night, many, including myself, did not sleep much, if at all. There was nothing to prevent one or even six men from rushing, grasping, and brandishing a weapon against the others. I cannot be the only one to have had thoughts of the relative merits of offence versus defence under the circumstances.

Where was Helen?

Days passed. It was indeed some kind of test,

or else a game, since they no longer brought us food. It would only be a matter of time before the natural divisions between the captives showed up. Six police from the South; nine white foreigners, *the blind*; several of their own people from the North whom we understood to be sympathetic to the opposition, or else some kind of criminals in their own right; and, six soldiers from the South captured some years ago, apparently, after a skirmish at a border village. One among them spoke English well. He told me that they were all thought to be long dead. *Of course we are dead, of course*, he insisted. I learned the southern word for *ghost*, which is how they describe themselves.

On the third day, I woke to a punctured scream and a sound I could not properly place. One of the knives had been self-employed—a *ghost* solider. An estuary of blood pooled, split, and ran in several directions, picking up dust as it slowed.

He lay among the knives. He was not moved. In the morning they entered. We were divided and interrogated singularly.

Did you kill the man?

No, I did not.

You?

No.

From then we were chained together at the leg. We would be made to work. Along with several of the police officers and two of my *blind* compatriots, we were put into a truck and taken deeper into the mountains. For several weeks we were forced to join their soldiers in clearing, excavating, and then building a barracks. The leader of the soldiers at the camp was the Colonel.

It became known that I was a physician. Perhaps at the Colonel's instruction, it afforded me some surprising respect from the guards and soldiers, many of whom had never experienced Western medicine firsthand. From time to time the Colonel asked me, in his broken English, to look at one of their number. Infected cuts mostly, which I would wash, stitch, or dress from a depleted first aid kit.

I did not know their word for antibiotic, if they even had one. I spoke to one of the *ghost* soldiers who I had come to know better than the others. I was struggling to communicate as I was providing care.

Can you help me translate? I asked him.

I will not help them.

There is a man who will die without antibiotics. He needs a hospital.

Better he die, than all those of my brothers he will go on to kill if he lives.

His logic of war was up against my professional ethics, which were still then intact. I looked him in the eyes and thought that I could play at his game, to get him to come around, so I said, When the day comes for you, I will not save you if *you* do not save him. But he had seen enough foreign doctors in his time.

Yes, you will, he said through his teeth in a grin.

Please, I said.

My brother's blood is on your hands, he said. Then he spoke in their shared language to the Colonel. I heard the word *doctor* and the word for *blind*, in a gentler tone. The Colonel looked at me. I pointed to the sick man and nodded with a serious look on my face, pointing right down at the expanding infected area. Then I pointed to the horizon and nodded. He had the man taken away; I do not know if he made it to a hospital for treatment in their territory on the other side of these mountains. I do not know if he lived, nor do I know if he went on to kill others.

Thank you, I said to the *ghost* soldier. What is your name?

Hector, he said. I am already a dead man but maybe that young man will grow to be a priest after this war.

You see, daughter. Life was not simple. But the *ghost* does live. Hector is my brother in the village. He and I speak of that sick man from time to time still. He says it was the first act of kindness he had ever shown *them*. Hector says now it was the beginning of his pathway to strength. If that sick man did die, it was not in vain. My brother did not go on to kill again.

In order that foundations could be laid, rock had to be removed. Blasts were set off with dynamite. Before each explosion, we were re-chained together and taken far enough away. Much shouting would occur before each detonation. On one such occurrence, we were removing rock and soil in buckets from the far side of a large mound, when the shouting began. We had not been chained and removed, as had been the case on each previous occasion. The explosion, so close, was a winding punch to the body and a bright, hot flash in my face. Then an eruption of rock shards, clay, and water covered my body.

As we unearthed ourselves, gasping for breath, several of us, myself included, could not see. In my ears, a roaring, a riot of tinnitus. And I could feel blood in my hair and on my face as my hands worked their way over my body. I heard the word for *doctor* in their language.

I regained partial sight by that afternoon. They left us chained to a tree. A man who had been with us since the hotel café was killed in the explosion. Unluckily he was smashed in the face with a large piece of rock. Our regular guard was injured too. I could not properly see, and there was nothing I could have done to help him. Others needed first aid. I was given some bandages and clean water and I dressed wounds as best as I was able, instructed people to apply pressure to wounds to stop hemorrhaging. As night fell my vision clouded further and my head felt light. We slept there, chained to one another. I realized I was concussed. At some point I drifted off.

In the night a panther came upon us. The blood must have attracted it. It circled. The guard was next to me. He seemed to have fallen asleep. Perhaps his injuries were worse than I'd thought. My eyesight was poor; all I could see were vague shapes and movements. I shook him awake. The cat pounced, the attacking noise of it primeval. One of our number must have kicked it off as it backed away, re-circling. There was shouting. Someone said they had a stick and would fight it off if it came back. The guard would not wake up. It was dark. I placed my hand on his neck. He was without a pulse. I reached down, impulsively, and felt for his handgun. It was beside him on the grass. Those I was chained to were now on their feet, so I stood.

The Colonel came bursting out of his tent, screaming orders. He fired his gun at the cat and into the air several times. Shadows and shapes came and went before me. There were other shots. I could hear the Colonel, his hateful voice. Every time I heard his voice I pictured him urinating on the bald man's body.

My daughter, in the heat of the moment, concussed, shots flying, while we were being attacked by a panther, I lifted the handgun and fired it in the direction of the Colonel. I then hurled the gun away behind me into the thick forest at our backs. I understood from those about me that the cat had darted away. Had I been seen firing the gun? I collapsed onto the ground.

In the morning I was unchained and was brought before the Colonel. He had been shot in the ankle, I was informed, and I was to treat it. My eyesight was cloudy and I had to place my face close to the wound to properly see it. The Colonel lay still. He had a first aid kit with creams and gauze. It was only a flesh wound and hadn't broken the bone. I dressed it. Nothing was said.

During the coming days, my eyesight did not improve. I could see up close if there was good light, and some shapes in the middle distance, but nothing beyond that. It was hard for me to labour, and I was taken away and made to help in the kitchen, cleaning pots and dishes after meals. At night I was re-chained to my group.

Once the building was finished we were moved about again, from the new compound to a tent barracks, and divided into smaller groups. Then, one by one, we were separated, assigned to different roles, soldiers, and camps. We would see one another from time to time on the road, occasionally made to work for a day together then not. We would exchange whatever gossip we knew, and would hungrily ask after one another.

After about a year, I was restricted to the larger camps. This was, I came to understand, due both to my poor eyesight, which limited my ability to work physically, but also it allowed the Colonel to extract the most from his only doctor. I treated wounds from battles and accidents. New and ever younger recruits continued to arrive in. I delivered three babies—all alive—birthed by local village women living with no men about—all husbands long dead or gone to fight. I could only assume these were babies born from a night of pleasure with, or violence from, a soldier. Each mother took the child to her breast though. Did they see these children as hopeful gifts? If they did, I do not know how, given the demands a baby makes of a lone mother.

Where were you and Helen, I wondered, other than in my dreams?

Then the war took a turn. We heard that foreign troops had come to help the other side stabilize the fighting. Both sides needed time to regroup. It was during this time of uncertain enemy lines that I was almost rescued. I saw the outline and shape of a jeep. Whispers around me were that it was driven by two white soldiers. They were coming toward the make-shift camp. Perhaps they were lost? Warning shots were fired and they spun around and retreated—not to return. But they saw me because one screamed out a one-word question: *English?* Was there surprise on their faces: a foreign white man, a prisoner among the enemy? Was word sent to embassies? *A foreign national was sighted!* Was I seen long enough to be described? Was it reported in the newspapers, picked up on the wires? Did I warrant news?

With my whereabouts now roughly known, I was quickly returned to the main compound.

Blind Doctor, said the Colonel, you are money when the time comes. Not now. You will go away.

I was sent to a new compound by the far coast, but still hidden in the mountains. Several other prisoners I knew, or had seen as I'd been moved about, were sent with me including my friend the *ghost solider*, Hector. Although I had been long detained, I had been kept on the move by the Colonel. So, I suppose, this is where my journeying ends and my years as a prisoner properly begin.

Let me tell you about my cell, my home.

The jail where they took me had been recently built—grey cinderblock walls on a cement floor. High up, just under the corrugated iron roofline, a single block had been left out, a hole acting as a window. I had been in work crews that had erected similar buildings in the mountains. The fighting was not as severe in the hills closer to the coast, the forest was denser, and the terrain was rockier with fewer roads. We'd heard that more jails were being constructed here because of this.

My cell's size was exactly two body-lengths wide by two body-lengths plus an extended arm long.

In the beginning they did not let us out. We could hear one another through the walls if we raised our voices. We learned to do this only at night when the guards were not about.

Doc? You there, Doc?

I am, I would say.

I want my woman, Doc, he'd say. Then he would go on, on and on in desperation, hollering out, I want to climb onto her and hump all the way across those mountains back to my village. I want to go home, Doc. Do you hear me?

I do, believe me, man. I do. It was all I could offer him.

He sounds crude, but how different was I? There was so much time to think about Helen. Hour after hour I would study the details of days we had spent together. Replay each one in my mind. Methodically work my way back through our travels. The places we had been, the camps, the crisis medical centres set up in fields, or schools, or bombed hospitals, the languid days off in cities in almost every continent.

I would choose a single day, even a meal perhaps, and recast it in my mind carefully, ensuring I would not rush and miss anything. Taking it as slowly as I could manage I would polish the details in my mind's eye, and then I would force myself to look harder, be sure not to miss anything. If I discovered a lost fragment of conversation, or a tension I'd never considered at the time, I would turn it over and over until it gave up whatever new gem it hid. A single day could now easily take two or three to properly unearth. This was how, especially at first, I kept Helen close.

In my cell there was a cot made with webbed, criss-cross black rubber strapping. There was also a bucket. This was switched out every two days.

On arrival they took my shoes from me—which were, by that time, the last remaining article of my original belongings. Some time ago I had been given an old yellow T-shirt and army surplus pants. My hair and beard were long during those years—especially uncomfortable when it was hot.

They fed us watery soup at midday. The distant flavour was powdered celery, I came to decide. Some rice was in it. Every few days cooked meat would come in the cup. Mostly white, it was boney and gamey but was a welcome relief from the almost constant hunger we faced. I took it to be a bird of some kind, maybe a gull or a pigeon they had caught or bought from a local trapper. Occasionally, cooked oily fish would be served with rice. I lost a great deal of weight, but when I was no longer doing physical work it levelled off.

In the late afternoon during the long summers, sunlight streamed in through the window hole. The light was toffee-coloured and warm and, if the wind blew in the right direction, I could smell the sea air—the brine of it.

In winter, wet and cold leeched in through the floor and walls, wind whistling in through the window. The first winter a hole opened up under one of the bricks at the floor to the outside. The rain falling off the roof was pooling against the wall and the bonding in the cement dissolved. One evening a field mouse poked its head in. I froze. It sniffed the air a moment, looking for danger before going back out the hole.

The next day I saved two grains of rice from the soup. I got right down onto the floor and put my face close to the hole, the two grains of rice six inches away and just in my field of vision. I waited but nothing. The next night I tried again. It came in, but saw me so close and scurried off. Next I tried leaving the rice and just listening. It came right at dusk and ate. Each night I began to inch my way closer along the floor until I could see it. If mice are capable of such a thing, we developed a trust. The twitch of it, tiny teeth chewing on the grain. The whole world, the essence of evolution, the feelings that one can have for another living creature played out for me as I waited and watched that mouse. Then one day it just stopped coming.

For an entire season the rain pelted down onto the metal roof, keeping me awake many nights. Whenever it stopped, I would fall into an immediate sleep, only to wake as the next wave of it pressed down against the building.

I grew more aware of smells and sounds, especially the subtle ones. My eyes never properly recovered from the explosion. I do not know which chemicals they used to make the explosives, but the flash-blindness I experienced was the result,

I suspect. What else could have caused permanent retinal damage? What were the chances that I happened to be looking right at the explosion? I am partially blind now. How fitting—some cruel irony, given our name in their language.

My daughter, there was a summertime game I enjoyed. The deep golden light would come pouring in the window hole. This beam of direct light came on cloudless days for a few short weeks once a year. If I stood on my cot, for about an hour I could hold my hands out in the shape of a cup and fill them with sunlight. Or I would take the sun on my face, imagining I was still sitting in the hotel's café, drinking my coffee, eating my brioche. Bread. Delicate strands of sweet, white bread. On two or three days every year, when the sun was at a certain place in the sky, the beam would inch down and reach low enough to touch my prick, or warm my ass if I perched on the cot. Please excuse the specificity.

If you are alone long enough, any new event is cause for joyful rapture.

The first night guard we had was a tall man with thick arms and a flat face and nose. Yes, his nostrils were what you noticed. He was a religious man, and spoke fair English. He was a Christian—less common in the North.

Doctor, I have Bible for you, to pray. I will take

it back tomorrow night. Was this a signal I was about to be executed? Or was he simply extending out his hand to me, one man to another?

It was winter at the time, and there was almost no light good enough in the cell for me to see words on the page, even at midday. I turned pages quickly until I found a story my eyes could rest on. It was Exodus, and baby Moses being saved from the Nile, his sister Miriam ensuring he survived to play the role he did. But oh my eyes were poor, the paper thin, and the type small. Before long I could see nothing clearly and so I simply held it. A book. *The* book.

I was never religious. That night alone with the guard's Bible did not change me. But I held it close, smelling the paper and the binding. A flower that had been pressed between the pages fell out. I ran it past my nose. Finally, it gave me the faintest hint. Lavender. Baby Moses and lavender.

You are a good man, I said, thanking the guard the next night when he came for it to be returned. He nodded. I understood that he had placed himself in some danger offering the book to me. You see, my daughter, there are strong hearts and kindness inside even the bodies of enemies. Of course, he was not my enemy. Neither side was.

HELEN WAS NOT THE ONLY one, the only memory, with which I occupied myself. The dreams of my father would begin with a word, or a sentence, as a voice speaking to me. His words were clear and they encircled me.

Home is accommodation. That was one of his aphorisms—their meaning would always twist this way and that. His voice was deep and musical and in my dreams it would be exactly as I remembered it. Not from the end when he was older, alone, depressed and sick, but from my childhood or teenage years, when he was vital and serious, and often on the television or radio.

I spent a lot of time listening to my father's voice. Curled up at the top of the stairs, he with friends in the living room, drinking wine and arguing, laughing. My father was always at the centre of things, pushing the line of thinking a touch too far, to see precisely where that line was crossed. It was a skill he made use of in the media later in life.

His voice boomed in my dreams, thundered, and sometimes the claps woke me—the sound of him and the smell of his boozy breath, his emphatic reasoning—taking some minutes to properly dissipate. You must hear the recordings of him I kept on tapes. I wish I could. I do not miss my possessions though. I have been here for so long I suspect I have mostly forgotten them. But I do miss playing those tapes. Following his death I would listen to them. They helped me keep him close and whole. They drew out my grief. Maybe that is why he comes to me in my dreams, still alive, full of spunk and reverence for ideas and solutions.

The tapes are with your great aunt Hesione. When I first left to work with Helen, I sold everything—car, furniture. I asked my father's younger sister to store a few boxes in her basement for me, the bare essentials with which I could not part. My framed degrees. A copy of a dissertation. Some old letters. Photo albums. Precious books—some written by my father. My college jacket. Perhaps other items too. And the tapes. These things are yours now. Go retrieve them. Listen to the tapes again for me, will you? Hear his voice and his mad way. I miss him. He would have been a wonderful grandfather.

In the summers my father wore a Panama hat, leather sandals with a buckle, and loose shirts. He would sit on the porch, drink an iced tea, and read. He always read. Newspapers mostly. Local ones written by the petty criminals, as he'd say, but he'd also read papers from around the world. Magazines and newspapers would land on our doorstep with a belated thud— sometimes weeks or even months after publication. They came from countries he both had, and had never, visited. You must read the hardened criminals too, he would insist.

Your grandfather did not care much for professional journalists, or journalism, as a rule. He would rail against their logic, their editorial cheap shots, their inflammatory positions. He would write letters to the editor aloud, narrating to his mythical secretary, Miss Jones, who was, presumably, somewhere nearby typing as he spoke.

Miss Jones! A letter, Miss Jones! This is how they would always begin. With a groan he would get out of his chair, either on the porch or in the living room depending on the season, and pad to the kitchen for coffee or booze, depending on the time of day. Miss

Jones worked unpredictable hours, as my aunt used to say when I was older.

Dear Editor, which, I confess, I address you as, sir, solely because it is your formal title and not because I see evidence of you editing anything. Dear Editor, your editorial column in today's edition was so weakly lobbed, my nine-year-old boy could easily have scored a double from it. He would, occasionally, work me in with a wink (if he suspected I was really listening). *While your recall of the prime minister's promise from his election campaign is correct, you have suffered an amnesia of convenience, self induced, to service your call for tighter fiscal control. The hand that gently guides your pen, i.e., your owner and master, today has applied enough pressure that from where I sit, it should rightly be called a proper squeeze. Are you getting all this, Miss Jones?* He would go on, peeling apart and laying bare the flaws in argument, occasionally thanking Miss Jones for asking him to clarify something he'd said. By the time he finished dictating, he would have made more coffee, or mixed himself a new drink, and would be settled back down into his chair. I never saw him actually write and send anything.

Yes, he loathed journalists as a rule. But as with most rules there were some exceptions, so those he liked he didn't just enjoy, he admired deeply. He would give them pet names and, if they were women, he would sing made-up love songs to them following his reading of an article that he found particularly stirring. If they were men he might talk to them aloud, as if they were sitting across from him at that very moment, his opinions being asked for as a contribution to the piece in question.

You must think of my father, your grandfather, as a crank, or a fool. He may have been those things. But, in truth, he was a brilliant man. A sought after economist, widely published, he guest lectured at universities and held increasingly important positions within the private banking sector and, ultimately, government itself, as the assistant deputy minister of finance.

When the government finally changed, he knew it was time to call it quits. He had made no friends on the other side. So the ranting he performed on the first floor of our house became his retirement hobby. I came to see his theatrics as something more deliberate. Either he predicted his role in the media, or was thoughtfully preparing for it through dress rehearsals. Other than some of his close friends or colleagues, or a group of graduate students, for many years I was his only real audience. Then, the country became his audience.

His voice came to me in dreams where we talked together. He would ask me how I am. *What are you thinking about in here?* And I would tell him of Helen, or of you. Mostly though, I would listen to him, the ebb and flow of his voice carrying his active mind to me. Sometimes I would wake and be so sure he was making deep sense of the world, interpreting whole patterns and structures for me, revealing their complexity. Yet if I tried to hold onto his words, what he'd been saying, they would not be there. I grew to understand that he came to me as a kind of vision—a spirit of conversation to keep me sane. He was a companion through deadened winter nights, alone in that cell hardly bigger than a closet, alone with only my ability to remember, to invent, to imagine. I am thankful I was given these gifts. In other cells, other men were not so fortunate. Their cries of desperation, pain, loneliness, went unheard into the night because of their void within.

When a mind is given no stimulation, time itself breaks down in ever smaller increments, eventually ceasing to properly be. Although living, you exist as one of the dead. What I now suspect to be whole years' worth of time would have passed and I saw no other person, other than the momentary flash of a guard's face as he handed me food. I gave up measuring days, or weeks, and settled down into myself. Moments from my past and moments yet to come, maybe never to come, all became my waking life. This is how you and I have been together. This is how I have preserved every precious moment with Helen.

As time dissolved, the structured way of living in the world did too. Was I still myself, Paris? Or was I some earlier or future version of myself? Was I just a continuum of a person, a man that had always existed down through the ages, like a roadway built long ago by an ancient civilization that never fell out of daily use? As each age came and passed, did the road survive, always receiving and guiding those in need of getting from one place to the other? If so, it is in this way that I survived and could be with you when we were kept apart, and know I could stay with you in the future. It was also how I could stay with Helen, long after that jeep disappeared down the mountainside.

Helen would speak in her sleep. I would lie awake listening to her talk nonsense, sometimes being able to catch single words, fragments of our day at work. But on a few occasions, late into the evening, I was awoken with a start. She had night terrors, unable to be consoled or calmed. She would rant and thrust with her arms, tearing at her hair. She did not mention these episodes the next morning and I did not bring them up. I told myself I did not want to embarrass her. But in truth I did not want her to stop having them. In this state, she was reliving events of her past. It was all I had of her history. So I kept this private, selfish access to myself.

In my cell, there was a dream I would have of

Helen. I came to see the dream as punishment for my betrayal of her, for breaching her privacy. In it she was a young girl. But it was an absurd dream. How could I conjure her? I was never shown photographs of her as a child. My sleeping mind had so little to work with. But I suppose girls look the way they do and I must have subtracted years from her, age retreating from her face, the fragile lines of experience becoming gradually shallower then smoothing out completely.

In the beginning of my dream, she was about eleven. It always began with her hanging upside down from a tree branch, the world about her a vibrant green. She then saddled it, legs swinging underneath her. She calls out to someone, her mother? She is at a picnic, or is at the end of her street, playing at a park. In the air her voice is thrilled, lyrical, chanting a song in minor thirds. Her freedom is so vast and filled with hope. Then the dream would pick up speed.

She was a teenager. Something had changed. She had experienced a new part of the world and it's a barb that has pierced her. My dream darkens. There has been a violation of her earlier hope. I sense she is in pain but I cannot reach her. She will not face me. Her beauty has already become the shaper of destiny, but instead of providing the world with radiant joy and the world responding in kind, something has damaged this circle of light. There is a void growing inward, deepening inside her. To counterbalance, she has gone on attack. She is filling with fight like a wounded domestic animal that will no longer trust its master.

Helen is against the wall in her high school gymnasium locker room. It is after school. I must tell it to you because it is the truth—my ghastly dream cobbled together from Helen's night terrors. I must tell it because I am not there to stop it.

He has Helen against a wall of lockers. Can you see her now? It is after school. Has she told you? Has she pressed you with the details, frightened you with them until you cried for her? I am not there to throw him down, to beat his face with my fist— yes, I might be a doctor, but I am still a man. She is being shoved against the lockers and her life is being altered, and once it has begun, the horrible hurt and his pitiful acting at it, it lasts until it suddenly stops and soon she is left there, alone with her wet face and bloody smears. And everyone knew. It carried itself about the school contagiously. But they had the details all wrong. The lust and desire were all his. She had tried to delay it once again, fighting him off with smart words and clever arguments, and in failing to do so, was left with nothing to say other than *please stop it* over and over, as if to forever remind herself that this was what she really meant.

This dream of violence and hate happened many times—far more times than did the night terrors on which it was based. I could not make the story stop or change. I could not stop him because I could not make myself enter into the dream, pull him away and belt his face. Men such as me are never there at the right time. This story is the oldest story in the world, the one that launches a thousand dark dreams.

=

I WAS AN UNWANTED CHILD. This I already knew, but after my father died, my aunt Hesione could no longer keep the secret. In short bursts, after glasses of sherry, she relieved herself of what she saw as my mother's crime. With many children already from previous marriages, my mother and father fell in love and were wedded within a year. My aunt let me know that she felt this union was doomed from the start.

Paris, you were to be the bond that was to keep them together, were her words. Yet shortly after I arrived, my mother's previous husband returned. After a year of going back and forth, she left my father. She and the other children moved away to be with their father. My father, furious, broken, and hurt, insisted on keeping me. He was in the throes of hiring lawyers and digging in, when my mother arrived with me, and simply gave me to him. In this manner, it was decided. It was the only kind thing she ever did for him, my aunt said.

My mother was not to be mentioned in the presence of my father. My aunt Hesione was the surrogate. But my father, for all his eccentricities, did his best to raise me. At the end of his life—while his pain was being managed—he had a burst of self-reflection and spoke of my mother. He confessed how much he had loved her. He told me what she wore on their wedding night. Imagine! He also spoke of a dream she'd had. He grabbed me by the face, quite hard for a sick, old man, and said, Paris, before you were born your mother dreamed she was giving birth to a flaming torch. Could I have named you anything but Paris after that? And he laughed and laughed: a wonderful sight to see a dying man laugh. It might have been the last time he did so.

Did she really have that dream? Did the name come first, and the dream was a story, a humorous idea later thought of, that was somehow twisted in his end-of-life state into something apocryphal? I'll never know. He really thought it was funny. A delightful joke he'd never before been able to share with me and it seemed to give him great pleasure in finally telling me.

═

MY DARLING, I HAVE NOT told you about the mass graves. Along with several other prisoners, I was forced to dig them during a strange few weeks where we were thrust back into the war proper, before being thrown into our cells and forgotten about once more.

I had been sleeping. It was spring and the light was warming once again and I found it easier to pass from this world into another one of dreams. My cell door clicked open and I woke. It was not time for food. A guard whose voice I did not recognize—I only knew two or three at that time—entered my cell and grabbed me by the upper arm.

Up, up, prisoner. Or perhaps it was: Come, come, prisoner that he'd said in their language. The *ghost* soldier, Hector, was directly across from me. I had learned he was once a political leader, a chief, or warlord of sorts, I suppose, from a town in the South. Disputed land, once his, now *theirs*. As a young man he attended university in the West. He enjoyed telling me about all the food he ate while he was away, hamburgers, spaghetti, and Froot Loops—those he'd loved the best it seemed.

Doctor, are you there?

Of course I'm here.

Just checking. Don't want you to think I've forgotten you! And Hector would laugh away to himself, enjoying the absurdity or silliness of whatever he'd just said, likely similar to whatever he'd said the day before. This is one way we survived, by checking on one another—in those rare moments when it was safe to do so.

Some of the guards were violent. They would beat prisoners. They did not permit calling from cell to cell. We usually reserved bursts of shouted conversation for late at night.

I will teach you some words now, Hector would announce, my lessons to be absorbed through cinderblock at night. He then would shout a word at me in his language, then in English, then the equivalent in *their* language. The North and South, as I was beginning to understand it, were dialects of the same tongue. So, *up* and *come*, sounded identical to my ears at that stage. They are, in fact, different words, but it takes some getting used to, for the nuances to properly reveal themselves. *Up, up, prisoner*, or *Come, come, prisoner* sounded almost the same.

Either way, this day would be a different sort. In the back of the truck we were jolted about. There were six prisoners and two soldiers with rifles. I joined my fellow prisoners in smiling uncontrollably. The light was bright and I could see a bit better than in the darkness of my cell. Hector was giggling to himself. We were so pleased at the chance to be outside our cells. We did not know where we were going. To our deaths? Or some other equivalent? To us this was a blessed excursion. So Hector and I rode down the mountain, bouncing into one another, our skin touching another human being's skin, eyes meeting eyes, the shape of one another's gaunt faces, hands with bitten nails and calluses from the cinder-block or from doing exercises or punching the wall just to feel some physical pain, we took it all in and we experienced joy. This was the first time we had been out of our cells since we first arrived.

My daughter, the problem of time persists. I really do not have a good idea of how long we'd been in there. Some years. Maybe two? They kept us so hidden at the beginning. We were a cross-section of political prisoners, men with either local or regional followings in the country, or else, as in my case, foreign nationals. What did we have in common? It can only have been that we were more useful alive.

At the foot of the mountains, with the sea maybe a mile away, we were unloaded and given buckets. We had been brought to work as diggers. The Colonel was there, walking from end to end, barking instructions, saying *hurry* in their language—I knew it was him, his voice came to me immediately. Suddenly he was in my face.

Doctor, he said. Join us. This is a hospital.

I knew he was lying. He knew that I knew it too. It did not matter. The Colonel sounded the same to me. When he drew close to my face and I could see him properly I noticed a weariness now around his eyes. The war had drained him of all right and wrong. If he was fighting for a noble cause, the deaths and ruin he had caused had bankrupted any initial goodness.

The clay soil was dark orange, the colour of rust and, as we got farther down, wet. At night we were made to sleep a fair distance away by the bank of a river, the water brown and ripe-smelling. Upstream, on the way here, we had passed a massive area of deforestation, burned ground and ashen stumps. We had seen men with hand tills turning the soil, preparing to plant crops. As the spring rain fell though, it washed the topsoil into the river. Dead freshwater fish bobbed and floated by on their way out to the sea. A fire of damp dung smouldered away, the smell of it peaty and thick. We were fed packs of aid rations, warming them in a pot of water over the few coals available. The silver packs had instructions and some words in English, and translations in other languages. I read and reread the English, making sure I knew all the words, that I'd not somehow forgotten anything.

This pack contains a main meal such as beef stew, chicken noodles, or spaghetti, along with crackers, spread, biscuits, condiments, and saline water. Each pack contains approximately 1200 calories.

We ate as we had not done in years. There was no talking. The pouches were licked clean.

There was screaming in the night.

Flame torches, hastily lit, flickered outlines of the surrounding foliage. Then a gun sent a bullet sizzling through the forest canopy, the sound of it hanging in the air. The prisoners around me huddled together and kept low. I could see only shapes, faint and fleeing, as they raced by with flames.

What, what? I asked those about me. None of the men answered—not even Hector. We did not sleep again. The soldiers were searching through much of the night for the escapees. In the morning the Colonel came to me.

Doctor, said the Colonel. I will kill these men who ran. I know you are blind. So I tell you.

For another four days we were made to carry bucketloads of wet clay out of an expanding pit.

It was much wider and longer than it was deep and we followed their instructions of where and how to remove the dirt. I could only carry half bucketloads, and not far. By the end of the fourth day I was exhausted and was unable to work. The Colonel locked me to the wheel of his parked jeep with a short, thin chain and padlock. He left me there with a box containing two aid packs, a street map of a city whose Spanish name I did not recognize, and the middle-half of a coverless paperback written in English. I believe this was his version of special treatment.

The spring rains had eased and days had grown hotter, and steamier. I was left there, unattended and largely unlooked at, for the next few days. I ate the rations slowly and purposefully, portioning them out over as long a period as I was able to stand. During the day I rolled underneath the jeep to get out of the direct sun, lying on my back in the dirt, the grease of the underside of the jeep only inches away from my face. I had no shirt or shoes. I read the novel. It was not one I'd ever read before, and neither the title nor the author's name were atop the pages. The story was about the First World War. Mustard gas and trenches. Running between the lines and horses being shot in the head due to superficial wounds, the beasts now burdensome. I caught snippets of the Colonel's conversation as he marched between the dig and the camp. I wondered why he kept me alive, why he treated me with some exception. This was not the first time. Was it still because I was a physician? Was it Helen?

So many nights in the cell I had combed the details of that final morning in the hotel's café—bougainvillea, brioche, Helen speaking with the interloping woman, the Colonel. I had examined it all exhaustively. There were no more clues, no gestures that might have given a new understanding of it all.

Helen knew she was not going to be detained with me, but did she know who she was talking to, the real identity of the leather vendor as the Colonel of the northern rebel army?

I have asked myself how your mother knew this. What, or who, or how did she come to know him?

Maybe you know. Maybe you pity me—how little information, or even how trusting I was, and I remained.

When I could no longer focus on the words in the novel, when the trench warfare became too much, when I no longer saw the point or found interest in staring at a map of a city I did not know, I thought of Helen again, of our last day.

It is time, Doctor, said the Colonel, kicking me gently in the leg.

I had been sleeping under the jeep. I crawled out and he unlocked me. I stuffed some final pieces of food into my mouth before he led me away. I kept hold of the book in desperation, hoping somehow I might be allowed to keep it.

You have become a dog, said the Colonel. He took the book from my hand and tossed it away.

What happened to Helen? I said to him. My voice came out unnaturally loud, and assertive. It was a voice I had not used in years. It was a doctor's voice. The one I perfected in medical school, the tone that instructed others to keep themselves together, the one that ensured everyone in the room—nurses, students, family members—knew that I was in complete control and that they must trust my authority, my skill. Now I had no control of myself. It came out of me as a kind of submerged spirit, rising from my broken being. The Colonel started. Then he put his face close to me. I could smell him, sour sweat and dirt.

Who? The woman I arrested you with? She is my own whore! he said. And then he laughed and patted me on the face as a father might do to a son who is not yet a real man. Then he said, I do not know. I have never seen her again. That time is long over. None of it succeeded. Now we are alone, on our own. It's better this way. You will see. We are winning. Soon the bodies will arrive.

It was not to be the foundation for a hospital but a shallow mass grave. I helped carry the stiffening bodies and toss them in. I carried only soldiers. I overheard the Colonel explain to another man that an ambush had been planned. On the other side of the mountains government troops had set up a base camp from which to launch new attacks into the mountains. But they were not yet prepared and did not know the terrain. The Colonel ordered the grave dug before he ordered the attack.

I make bodies disappear, he said to the man. I am magic.

I don't know the number exactly, but perhaps fifty bodies were tossed, some limp others stiffened, into the pit that day. Petrol was poured on and the outdoor cremation began with a burst of light and heat flaring into the sky.

The corpses were still smouldering as we tied rags around our faces and began dumping the dirt back on. We worked much of the afternoon and into the next day until a spongy mound had been made. I vomited up the last aid pack I'd eaten. I've never had a reaction like that; maybe I was suffering from heat stroke. During this time the Colonel was called away.

Once finished, we stooped before our work, leaning, beaten. Hector said the dirt mound was a blanket stretched over a fat man's stomach; it hides nothing. I imagined how this would look from the air, a graze of fresh earth in the forest. Does a satellite photograph of this exist? If I was not to be saved, I still hoped for evidence of this crime to survive.

Doctor, one of the *blind* men said to me in the truck on the way back to our cells, perhaps all our digging will prevent cholera at least.

Dead bodies don't spread disease. That's a myth.

The man remained unconvinced, saying, Who are you anyway, talking to that dog the Colonel! You're not a doctor, are you? Liar. And the man then lunged at me, grabbing my neck and squeezing. A guard pulled him off and pointed his rifle at the man for some time. I hadn't registered trouble in his voice when he first spoke. Maybe it was my tone. Had I used my physician voice again? Did it suggest to him that I had everything in hand, and that I was to be trusted to get us all out of this? If this were the case, then his reaction was understandable.

By that night we were all back where we had begun, alone in our cells. Through the window hole I could see a fuzzy blur—the moon. It was the rarest event, just a piece of it, creeping into the frame, adding an unfamiliar light glow to my square of night sky. Fuzzy. The word reminded me of Helen eating a peach. It was on a day off and she'd said that all she really wanted in the whole world was a peach. I went out into the streets and spoke to person after person until I found a market. About me were merchants selling grains and mangoes, rice and tubers—but no peaches. It was such a long shot.

What's wrong with mister, why so sad, eh? said a woman behind a stall. She was young and pretty. I said I was hoping for a peach. And I smiled at her, not even knowing if she understood what I said.

We have better than that here. Take this, try it, try it. And she put an orb into my hand, about the size and colour of a tennis ball. You believe me? I smiled and said I did. I paid her for it and left.

It's all I could find, I said, and told Helen the story with a shrug.

Well, let's see, she said, and ripped open the skin. The flesh inside was white and stringy looking. She bit into it and made a face of delight. Always trust local knowledge of God's best work, she said. And then added, Thank you, Paris. That was kind.

==

MY FATHER KNEW WHAT IT was to live alone. I think he would have understood the way my mind loosened while I was in captivity. I don't just mean that he lived alone as a single man, all those years after my mother left him. Arguably, he had me around, and his work kept him company too. I mean the decade before his death. The years he spent following his on-air incident, after which he retreated to a cabin on a property in a remote part of the country.

My daughter: when it is left to itself, a mind evolves. Why parse matters here? The mind. The body. The self. Me. I.

At the outset, I was frantic to remain . . . what is the right word? Aware. Let's use that word. I was determined to stay aware of who and where I was. I was a prisoner of war—of sorts. Caught up in a conflict in which I had played no part, owed no allegiances to one side or the other. I had not been charged with a crime—not that the rule of law had even been in play. For all I knew, as the days passed, the time was shortening until a morning would arrive and my cell door would be sprung open by government soldiers or Special Forces from some Western nation having parachuted in—as they do in movies—to rescue their own. If this were to happen, and I was to look back on such an event having had occurred, I wanted to make sure I was still aware, and had been able to stay mentally fit.

I have seen the way my rescue would play out enough times on television. The narrative goes like this: after being flown to some nearby foreign military air base and having shaved and taken a quick shower, looking frail and tired, I would deliver a command performance at a press conference. I would say that my captors did not harm me, and that I was grateful for the work my government did to safely secure my release. That is how the release story goes. If it cannot go like that, it does not go on television at all.

But maintaining a sound mind, one that is always prepared to be rescued, is itself the delusional state. Free or incarcerated, each man has only a limited time on this earth. How you live it within your allotment, and the given circumstances, became an all-important idea to me. I could not afford to waste my days waiting for some new state of military-designed reality to drop down from the sky.

My father suffered from severe depression. I did not know this growing up as a child. He would simply drift away from me, and the world around him, for months at a time. I learned how to take care of myself. When I was young, my aunt would take me in. As I got older, I felt it my responsibility to take care of him. I would lie for him in increasingly clever ways, and wait for him to return. As I saw the warning signs, I would insist he take a vacation. This was code between us. And he would yank me out of school and we would get in the car and drive and drive. Usually to someplace warm, where we'd stay put until things came to pass for him.

When we couldn't get away, when he still needed to teach or work at the bank, or during his later years in government, I would do the shopping and pay bills. I would make him dinner and bring it to him, getting him out of bed to go to work if I was able, or making him call in if I wasn't. I later learned that many of his colleagues thought he was an alcoholic and would cover for him. One of his closest friends told me at his funeral that it wasn't until he'd had his public breakdown that he'd put it all together.

His public breakdown. That's what it was. Why do the media exploit mental health incidents? I

believe it is because they can just report the facts—
leave out all innuendo. They can objectively report
someone behaving impossibly improper or irrational. It requires no injected sensationalism for it
to be enticing.

I was a medical student on a placement at the
time and so I didn't see it occur. Only later did I
watch it after my aunt called me at work to let me
know. It was a typical live-to-air political debate
show. He'd been doing them for several years.
They loved his biting commentary and his fearless
insider insight. His career was in the past, and being
a political pundit was simple enjoyment for him.
On this day, a particularly pointed argument broke
out, and his opponent took a personal swipe. You
could almost see my father breaking. He sounded
coherent at first, but his statements began to make
less sense. He accused his opponent of lying, of corruption. The moderator stepped in, and for whatever reason the producer did not go to commercial.
My father then began a rant that included descrip-
tions of the man buggering a former premier and
bribing officials in the ministry of finance. The man
just laughed and goaded him on, and the moderator only desperately tried to rein it in. Then my
father had stood and punched the man in the jaw,
knocking him right over.

My father was charged with assault. The media

played and replayed the clip. His opponent cast himself as the victim of a vicious tyrant. Public relations people employed by the opposition party, which my father largely supported, came to his rescue and provided the media with doctors and psychiatrists to properly characterize this for what it was: a breakdown. Dad was never convicted. He issued a public apology and detailed the ways in which he was now getting treatment. It all went away. And so did Dad's beloved retirement career.

He sold the house and moved to the cabin. I tell you this sad story for a reason. Your grandfather knew how profound it was to be forced to remain solitary. The shame he'd felt was acute. He felt he could never see people again. However, he underestimated the happiness found in memory and imagination. He learned the staying power of it. I know because he allowed some of us to visit him up there from time to time. And on these occasions he let me know what he'd learned about it, about himself. After weeks of not speaking to anyone, no radio or television, a trip into town for food was about all he'd do if he'd completely run out of everything. Was it penance? I don't think so—he was too much of a crank. He'd simply learned to find pleasure in isolation.

I found pleasure in isolation too, but not until I discarded the notion that I would be saved and that my time here in this cell was temporary. Once I let that hope go, I became free to live. Those were the hours we spent together, my daughter. Those magical years. No one can take them from me. First, moment by constructed moment, they were my imaginings. My inner life kept pace with how it would have, should have, been. And now they are my memories. The broccoli quiche you refused to eat. The first sunfish you caught at the lake. They are no less real to me, no less important, than if they had really happened. Can you accept this? Do you think me as poorly off as my father? I hope not. You are real, and we have lived a rich life. I will die happy. Is that not all a man can ask?

=

WHY DID YOU BECOME A doctor? asked Helen. We were on a break between surgeries, the last was a hand amputation of a man who had been attacked with a bush knife. There was no saving it. Not out here. Not with my skills. We had seen enough victims like him on that assignment. Lawlessness and violence played itself out each night in the scrubland surrounding the city. Young men mostly, drunk on the strong yeasty beer and fuelled with the anger only joblessness can incite.

For the money, I said and laughed.

Seriously, she said.

It's just how I see myself. It started young. I had this urgent desire to take away pain. Does that make any sense?

Yes, it does, she said.

Why did you become a nurse?

When I'm providing care to another person, I am not feeling anything myself and I want that. It's a narcotic.

That country was in turmoil, its political structure had dissolved. Foreign troops were in place; the peace was thin. We did not stay long, for reasons I never did understand. The needs were real and ever present, but Helen was anxious to be re-posted. I went along with her.

The night before we were to ship out, we ate at one of the still functioning restaurants in the capital. It was in the safe zone, heavily guarded, and Western humanitarian workers were the ones mostly populating the few thriving shops and stalls.

Why do you follow me? she asked as we sat eating.

Are you really asking me that?

My daughter, at first I responded the way you'd expect. Helen was the most beautiful woman I'd ever known. Her dedication to her work and to healing people was profound. I said as much, but then I stopped. She wasn't asking me something. She was telling me something: her description of nursing as a narcotic against the self, her devotion to God. This work, the rip and tear, the violence of the medicine we were performing. She was running from herself, from some deep wound. Why was I making it harder for her to remain numb? This was her real question.

At that restaurant, steaming bowls on the table, vegetables and spices and meat, the night warm and swirling about us, and the familiar throb of danger in the air, I finally put some of it together. And my instinct was what it always was: to take the pain away. And so I tried. And tried. I did not let her go. I did not respect her deeper wish, to be alone and to forget her pain, her past. I thought I could cure her by loving her. I thought I could fix things, bring her back to a normal life and find happiness. Was that the wrong decision? I have never believed so. Not for one day in that cell did I deny her. How could I, when she gave me you?

=

SOME OF US WERE MOVED into new cells after we'd dug the mass grave. I was not. I had long understood that not all cells had a window, that prisoners who spoke the local language were largely not given windows and, I supposed, the opportunity to shout out to villagers passing by. In the past months many of the villagers had returned, women mainly but some children, and their cries of laughter floated through the hole and down to me, to my ears bringing a gorgeous ease, filling me with desire to again be with others.

In the moments driving to and from the village on our way to the dig, I had been too stunned by the raw light for my eyes to make out anything much except the outlines of buildings.

What do you see? I'd asked the *ghost* soldier. Hector knew my eyesight was poor. He could tell by my urgent voice—I would want to know, for later—what did the village around my jail cell look like? He understood my need, and leaned into me so I could hear him.

There are buildings made of mud, Hector said as we bounced down the hill. There is a stand over there selling fruit and live birds that have been caught in the bush. That is where they would congregate to leave to go to market in the nearest large town. Can you see that white building? That is where they pray.

How many of them are there? I asked.

Not many. Only women and small children, but it's enough to call a village. There are ruins about too. Former houses and other structures, burned or fallen down, left over from before the war. This was a much bigger place once. Maybe it will be again.

It will take the war to end first.

If there are any men left alive in the whole country, they will come looking for places like this.

Why? I asked him. Because it is safer up here in the mountains? Good hunting?

No, no. Hector was laughing. Because there are so many good women here, man. If I get out, I will come back here. I will father the whole next gener-ation of this village. And he laughed some more at himself, at us, alone, in captivity, helpless.

=

WITH THE CELL MOVES THAT followed the digging, I had a new neighbour. He did not have a window like me. I did not know who he was, who the man was that scratched on the floor with a rock or piece of tin. He was trying to communicate with me. But I had a lot on my mind.

It was the rainy season and the winds were coming in stronger than ever before off the sea, hours away. The air was brackish. The concrete dust became damp and stuck to me. I was a portrait of myself in grey watercolour. The guards provided Hessian sacking for us to cover ourselves against the cold at night. I was bitten by the ticks it carried, and hunted them for days. The scratching persisted. At night I called out to him. Stop it, I said. But there was no response.

During the day it was not cold, but the water seeped in and a rust trickle from the rotting rebar in the disintegrating concrete floor wound its way through my cell. The hole where the mouse once entered now allowed in a rivulet that flowed under my cell door.

Still the rains continued, still the scratching continued. The rains came down, pulsing into the night, making rhythms on the corrugated roof. It came down so forcibly at times that there was nothing to do but to concentrate on it, the pelting, with no beginning or end, just more water.

On he scratched. He was trying to teach me his language. A longer pull. A short tap. Two drawn-out taps. Not Morse code. He seemed to have devised his own lexicon; he was insisting I learn it. I had a piece of concrete that had come dislodged from my floor. It did not make the same sound as the metal he was likely using. Still, I tried. I began by copying him. I heard two short taps. When I repeated this, my first attempt at participating, he rapped his metal piece against the wall higher up. I took this to mean applause or approval.

I am a two-year-old learning to talk. I am illiterate and respond to positive feedback by repeating success again and again. After some days I have successfully repeated various combinations and patterns back to him. He is patient. We have the time. Tap, drag, drag, tap-ti-tap tap.

I made letters in the wet concrete dust and began to ascribe taps to each. I attempted to spell words. This was not successful. We tried other ways. I believed he had invented a system that he wanted me to learn, and I was willing, but I couldn't crack the code. I didn't understand the referent for each noise or series of noises.

Was he tapping words out in English? I had assumed he was a foreigner. I began to doubt this. If he was one of the political prisoners from the South and was working from different phonetics, well, this would never succeed. I was frustrating him. I was frustrated. I just hammered slowly against the wall for a time. I thought of the slow chant of a bored or frustrated crowd at a soccer stadium, hoping for some action in the play. He continued on tapping and teaching. I stopped. Was I trying to learn a language of the mad? With no light, and in this wet, perhaps he had lost his mind. He had a perfectly logical series of sound patterns that meant words, a grammar of understanding—but was all nonsense to me.

He continued for days. So did the rain. Scratching and tapping. Talking and instructing. He copied my slow tapping from time to time, trying to rouse me. I thought of this in general terms, discarding the specifics of what he was trying to say, or teach. He was a man tapping on a wall, desperately.

He was utterly alone and believed he had a way out of this. He did, and he did not.

The way outside was to look further inside. The rain, the man tapping—both distracted me from my life with you, daughter. My comfortable, carefully considered life that was more precious to me than managing to exchange a few simple, scratched-out words with my co-prisoner.

Several days later the tapping faltered, and then finally stopped. On my cot I watched the rain-water run through the mouse hole and wind its way along a crack in the cement floor. I climbed off my cot, putting my face right down next to the water so I could see properly. I was right, it had turned red. The rivulet was blood. I cried out for the guard. I screamed and cried out. Eventually he came and I showed him, pointed to next door.

The only scenario I could imagine was that having failed in using the metal against the wall to communicate he used it across his wrists. That night I called out to the *ghost* soldier.

I do not know who it was, man, Hector said. Maybe they put him in there when we were away digging.

I was never able to find out anything more.

DAUGHTER, I WANT TO TELL you about a dream. I am at a farm. A large brown cow is alongside a wood fence that is painted bright white. The dream is still. Breeze and time is measured in the breaths I take. Do you think this is an image from when I was young? It is invented, or else it is one of those image dreams that many people have, and means something to those psychologists who study such things. After a time a woman comes in from somewhere and stands beside the cow. She pivots toward me. Her hair is auburn and wet. She smiles and walks toward me. The cow bobs its head down and takes up a mouthful of grass, begins to chew. It all appears completely natural and sure. The woman's shirt is perfectly ironed. She simply comes toward me. She never arrives but does get closer, staying in the middle distance, purposefully walking.

She talks to me in some versions of the dream. She makes simple, conversational statements that seem unconnected to anything. *That's fine with me.* Or, *Let's try that tomorrow.* I assume there must be more to our conversation, and that I retained these phrases because I had woken up soon after she'd spoken, for whatever reason. Why the cow? I do think there are other matters she speaks to me about though.

Do you have this dream?

My father had a similar dream to this. His was a horse, but the woman seemed to be the same. We would always tell one another when we'd had it. I always enjoy it because of this connection and if I have it close to dawn, I hold onto the feeling it gives me, let it swim about me freshly in the morning. The tone of her voice is as familiar as snow.

I thought I'd tell you about it, as if you and I were having tea, and you'd shared a story of a dream with me, and it was my turn to respond. And also knowing that your grandfather would want me to see if it was somehow passed along to you.

=

THE NOISES FROM THE SURROUNDING village became more frequent. I sensed a change in the country. It began with the sound of a voice. Far off, drawing closer. A conversation began and others joined it. I listened hard, picturing the person from whom the voice was coming. It was a man.

For reasons I did not then know, a few men had begun to move back into the village, joining the women and children. Their deeper voices carried to me through the night especially as they sat in groups around a fire, with talk and the crack and hiss of drying wood.

The men would sing as they worked, perhaps repairing houses or civic buildings. But their presence altered the confidence of the other people. They were able to once again be properly, safely alive. Did this change I felt in the air, the electricity of a new day, mean something for me too? I had no real knowledge, I told myself. Just snippets of laughter and song that floated in on the wind, local people going about their business. Still, I could not ignore that until recently there was no real village life. The settlement had been gradual. Tentative calls from one woman to another, a baby crying. Then more women and children. Then a few men. And the sound of trucks coming and going delivering food or water.

One day I received no food cup at the usual time. Instead, I heard a man's voice on a megaphone. If I had spoken their language better I might have caught more than the few simple words I did—which did nothing to reveal to me the purpose of the announcement. But as I listened to the faint rise and fall of it, the tones of appalled outrage then of assurance and trust, I knew exactly what was happening. My heart rushed at the recognition. And then, if I was still in any doubt, applause spilled forth from the villagers. This was a candidate. There would be elections. Perhaps there would be change. Then, almost as quickly, I considered the possibility of its opposite being true. Perhaps there would be more of the status quo, or worse, violence. This was all conjecture, but I did have some evidence after all. The guards arrived later in the evening with our food. They appeared no different.

Soon after I'd overheard the speech, the emissary arrived.

My name is Claude, he told me. His English was faltering, but we were able to converse. He asked who I was, where I was from. I drew his face close to my own.

My eyesight is poor, I told him, seeing the first white face in so long, now up close. Blue eyes. A receding hairline. Narrow nose. Thin lips, clean shaven, slightly cleft chin. Claude, I spoke his name several times to myself, to hear the ring of it, to see him nod in agreement, that he was real, that I was speaking it correctly.

I only have a few minutes, he said. We must talk quietly—the guard is listening and will report on what he understands of our conversation. I am with an NGO. We are the only ones who stayed in the field here. We paid the Colonel bribe money. No others would. Sometimes you have to do what you have to do.

I nodded.

We had heard rumours late last year that there was a white doctor being held. We couldn't believe it.

There are others too, I said. A few other foreigners.

No, he said. They are no longer here. I have

been in all the cells today. There are only four of you here. The others are former leaders of the previous opposition, and a priest.

I saw them before the rainy season. We were forced to dig a mass grave together.

Where?

Two hours down the mountains. Close to the sea.

We found it already. We know about it. How many bodies, do you know?

Fifty, I think. Soldiers. Maybe a few others?

We did research on who had been thought killed when the fighting broke out. You were one of those who we surmised may still be alive—if this rumour we'd heard was true.

I'm glad it was true, I said, and tried on a smile. He returned it.

There are to be general elections next month. The government is a ruling junta. You know this?

Tell me everything, please.

The Colonel no longer has the will of the people. He has spent all the country's money on munitions. The soldiers have abandoned the army because they are no longer being paid. The opposition is organized and the Colonel agreed to call an election. It will be observed, but most of us think it will be a sham. He is doing all this to secure new money from oil proceeds in the North. We know he wants to mount a new campaign to dampen the growing strength of the southern opposition. That's where things stand.

What can you do for me?

I have bribed three officials to get in here today. I do not know if there is anything I can do yet, but at least we know you are alive. Efforts to negotiate your release can begin, if you wish them to. But I would not advise it. I believe we should wait and see how the political situation develops first. Best case, the Colonel's army simply falls.

In the meantime, it is our experience that once political negotiation begins, there is every chance you will be moved again and again, and we may lose you. Or negotiations may not succeed and the Colonel will kill you if you are not worth money to him. Either way, sometimes these things go public and the media gets hold of them.

There are four or five independent journalists in the capital right now, covering the election. Two of them know the country well, and know that this is a real human rights story. If he falls, no one knows the totality of what we will uncover, how many bodies. There are some estimates of fifty thousand. . . . You don't look surprised.

No. What about my country, my organization? Do they know I am here?

Paris, I can tell you that not long after you were

captured the humanitarian agency you worked for was shut down. You'll recall its religious affiliation?

It was Christian.

It was bankrolled by an evangelical church, yes? On the surface they operated in much the same way as many other aid agencies. The fieldwork they did was among the bravest. Many good clinicians, such as you, gave themselves over to the work. Sadly, the backing church itself got into trouble. A scandal. Embezzlement and fraud charges levelled at the leaders of the church and this extended to the executive director of the agency too. I can't recall all the details. In any case, the aid work ceased almost immediately. I mention this to you because if you feel abandoned by the organization, well, you were not alone. Of course none were quite literally as abandoned as you were. As for your government, they have nothing on the ground here. They are of no use to you or me.

It's time for me to go. I will do what I can, and will be back when I am able. Stay strong, Paris.

Please, I asked him, there was . . . a nurse with the organization. I must know what happened to her.

I quickly gave him what details of Helen I could. I even mentioned you, my daughter, that Helen had been pregnant at the time, in case that helped him locate her.

Tell Helen I am alive.

He said he knew people, and would try. He reached into his pocket and pulled out a piece of tin foil unwrapping it carefully.

Chocolate, he said. Here.

And then he left. I sucked the small piece, the sweetness and memory of it overcoming me before both dissolved in my mouth, until everything was exactly the same as it was before he came. Just myself in my cell, with you, with my happiness, and with the growing sounds of village life drifting in through the window hole. You were swimming in a pool today with friends, I thought, and went about picturing you in my mind.

=

THE MESSAGE OF MY FATHER'S illness had been delivered by donkey. The old man who was employed to shuffle supplies and missives from the organization to us came on donkey every few days. It was an effective mode of transportation in that region. Having clopped his way to our field operation, the man shuffled over to me and handed me a manila envelope. Inside it was a printout of an email. The man stood waiting as I read.

The email was short and from my aunt. She had sent it to the organization's headquarters for urgent forwarding.

Paris,

> *Your father's condition has progressed.*
> *It's time for you to come home. He was*

admitted to the local hospital with respi-
ratory problems. He's been discharged,
but the doctor there told him it would
not be long. You know your father. He
did not want to stay in the hospital. So
he's back home and has a hospice nurse
coming in several times a day. He is on
oxygen and pain medication and is com-
fortable enough. I have been up and back
to his place several times now. He's been
talking about you a lot. I know he's dif-
ficult, but it's time now.

—Your loving aunt, H

I had to finish the three cases we had before us—one woman was losing blood and needed urgent care. That was my decision. I asked the man with the donkey to wait a few hours. In the time that it took me to treat the patients, another few showed up. I saw them too. We closed the clinic for the day as the sun was setting and I set off atop the donkey, my backpack strapped on as well, the man walking alongside.

I will be back as soon as I'm able, I said to Helen as I departed.

It is right that you are going, she said.

I'll miss you terribly.

We'll manage here, or wherever we are, well enough.

I was not at my father's bedside for almost four days. I rode the donkey, on and off, for half the night. I could not get to the airport until the morning, and then could not get a plane for another twelve hours. I changed planes twice more before I made it. I was beyond exhausted from the trip, but could tell Aunt Hesione was relieved I'd arrived. I slept at her place, in the room where I'd stayed so often as a child, still the same burgundy and blue quilt on the bed, the same chest of drawers unmoved where she'd kept a stash of my clothes and a few toys. In the morning we set out for my father's cabin.

I wasn't ready to see my father like that. My daughter, it's not what you think. It wasn't a son's irrational fear of his father's death and the sadness, or deep well of other emotions that would inevitably surface. I'm a doctor. I'd had time to consider this day from the time we first learned of his cancer and secondary problems. I knew he was going to get sicker. And had been doing that, if slowly, for two years. I was expecting all that.

I wasn't ready though to see him frail and withering, on oxygen and with a pain pump, because I just hadn't seen palliative care done in this way, which is to say properly, in some time. It wasn't my father I was confronting at all. It was me.

I was witnessing the choice I'd made in how I'd been practising medicine in a personal way.

I'm ashamed to admit, but my first thought was about myself. In chasing Helen across the globe, in doing this humanly important work in developing countries, I was letting my Western clinical skills erode and not staying current in clinical research. I'd trained so hard to master all this. Given everything for it. How much longer could I continue in the field before I would not be able to return? It would not be tomorrow or even next year, but some day. Would Helen ever give up her work? Would I be willing to never practise again in a proper hospital? It could come to that. A choice was coming: my work, or Helen and her work.

Four days before I'd removed a young man's foot due to it being all but severed by a machete in a territorial street fight. My father's cancer, irrationally, struck me as a luxury. His gradually managed death seemed decadent. I'd been practising medicine in countries where, if someone beat the odds and lived long enough to develop cancer, it would likely not be diagnosed. No imaging, no labs, no oncologists, and in essence no real way to treat. It would just run its course, metastasize to the brain, liver, and he'd die the way people had been doing since the beginning of time—from being old. But that was the rarity. As I bounced from country to country the death I saw mainly took the young. I saw either the effects of war, such as gunshots or knife wounds, or else the effects of poverty and malnourishment: rickets, typhoid, Ebola, cholera, tuberculosis. The idea of passing away with well-managed pain right up to the end made me irrationally angry at the inequity in the world.

Dad, it's me, Paris, I said as I approached the bedside. He turned his head toward me. It was still him. His face up close made my initial, reactive anger subside. Within minutes I calmed down. I became a son again, not a physician. Here was my father. This was the end. Here was his face up close. A face I had known since the beginning of my own life. And now it would be around no longer. I reached out and touched his cheek, his forehead. His skin was yellowy-grey with jaundice. He'd not been shaved in a few days and his whiskers, white and thinly spread now, grew out of his neck, chin, and jawline.

My aunt and I sat with him for about a week. We talked in his presence. She told stories about my childhood. He was in and out of consciousness. He told stories for the first few days. At one point near the end I made him smile. I'd been reading the daily newspaper to him with scant reaction, but I sensed he was enjoying the sound of my voice and the distraction of the news. In the middle of a report I stopped.

Miss Jones, are you there? Dear Editor, I began. While I address you as Editor, I would remind you that with that it comes an obligation to actually correct mistakes in the articles you print, namely, the difference between *sole* and *soul*. I looked at Dad. The corner of his mouth was stretched and opened in a slack smile. I'd evoked his muse. His always adoring, willing, and available Miss Jones. As I saw his smile then, I realized something I never had before. She was real. Perhaps her name was not Miss Jones, but perhaps it was. She was not a fictional character. She was a real person he knew, not someone he *pretended* to talk to as he thumped about the house showing off. He had really been showing off. He had been practising in front of me, not to impress me, but to impress her. Who was she?

My daughter, we will never know. But it pleased me to gain this insight at the end. That his heart did open itself for another woman. For you, Miss Jones, whoever you were.

I woke from a nap in his wingback chair and knew he'd stopped breathing. I called out to my aunt, who was making dinner. We stood beside him holding hands.

The days that followed were a blur of funeral arrangements and flowers, and obituaries and old friends phoning with sympathies. I emailed Helen the news, sent it via head office. The executive director wrote right back and told me the team was in transit. A mudslide had covered a village in a neighbouring country. I'd seen it in the newspaper yesterday that I read to my father. I told her I would be willing to join them at the end of the week. Could I come sooner? she replied. I'll do my best, I said. Another incremental decision had just been made.

At the funeral my father's long-time boss, friend, and former minister of finance gave the eulogy. He cited many of my father's accomplishments as an economist, policy maker, and teacher. He talked indirectly—he was delicate, not obtuse— about my father's fight with depression without mentioning the on-air incident. Notwithstanding, the incident *was* what was widely dragged out and rehashed by the media as his death became publicly known. My daughter, may I share with you something? One unexpected thing the minister of finance said was this:

> *Priam was a dedicated family man. I can tell you, as we worked late into the night in the lead-up to a budget or whatever else was the pressing issue for the government of the day, Priam always ducked away for an hour. Got to tuck in my son, he'd say. He was not asking for permission*

the way some might. He knew where his priorities lay. Of course his son Paris is now a grown man and a notable physician working on the starkest front lines of delivering health care to our world's most vulnerable populations in deplorable conditions. I spoke to Priam as recently as a month ago, and it was of Paris, and your important work, Doctor, that he talked about most. There was never a prouder father of a son.

In the receiving line afterward, there were tears and laughter—many people I did not know but who had worked with and for my father over the years, and admired him greatly. I scanned the faces of the women. What would Miss Jones have looked like?

Later that evening I returned to the city to catch a flight out, then I would rendezvous with an aid convoy heading to the crisis zone. With Helen at my side, I worked virtually around the clock for the next two weeks. That was the final assignment before we ended up in this country, working at the camp, retreating to the hotel and its café, together.

=

FIGHTING BROKE OUT. THE SOUND of gunshots cracked sharply, echoing against the cinderblock walls of the jail. They were not far off, close to the village. For a time they would taper off, then again the firing would erupt. Gradually it came closer, further up the mountain, closing in on the village. Was this related to the election?

The shots continued sporadically into the night. I do not know if the villagers remained in their houses, tending to their fires and feeding their children, or if they fled on foot, deeper into the mountains. Mealtime was missed the next day. And the next. Cries began from other prisoners. Hunger set in deeper with me, more angrily, than I'd ever recalled. I joined them in screaming out for food. Our cries went unanswered.

By day four I felt weakened and lay on my cot.

We had been forgotten. Other men still raged. The shots came and went in bursting clusters. Bullets hit the outside wall of the prison. Abruptly the sky grew dark and a storm let rain down hard on the roof. The fighting inched closer. The storm was intense but over quickly, leaving a purple then yellow light bruising the piece of sky I could see through the hole high in the cell wall. The gunfire continued for another day. Finally, a quiet grew.

The stillness was broken about dusk by the sound of keys in the prison hall. Doors were opening and voices came alive. Men were being set free. Opposition soldiers had arrived. I heard the dialect of the South, men speaking as Hector did, as they did in the town from which Helen and I had been taken. Not all the doors were opened. I heard the word for *blind* outside my door. And the word for *doctor*. And the word for *no*. Repeated several times, *no, no*.

Please, I said.

There were other shouts too. Others were not set free. Political prisoners from the North, perhaps. I had not eaten in days. Trucks and motors came and went outside the prison. There was much shouting in the village. I could hear the voices of women now, crying out for the children. Some men too. Voices of opposition soldiers. Trying to communicate. On my cot I lay down preparing to die. The prison was no longer staffed. If it took more than another week for them to check each cell, I would not survive. The *ghost* soldier knew it too and began screaming to me.

Doctor. Call out your window, Hector said. But I lay on my cot without the strength to fight any longer.

The retreating government soldiers, prison guards, set fire to the surrounding forest as they made their retreat. With all the water that had fallen, the brush did not ignite well, but they must have dumped out petrol. Thick smoke bellowed over the town, and into the window hole of my cell. Elsewhere prisoners screamed. A kind of madness then took over the few of us left. I drew short breaths, prone on my cot.

Smoke inhalation, or the early stages of starvation, made my body begin to shut down, preserve itself and will itself to live for as long as it was able. The visions I had were complicated and unrecoverable to me afterward.

Some of the prison buildings were burned. Opposition soldiers returned and took control of the prison the following day. I remained imprisoned, mostly unconscious. Whatever accusation or charges against me, real or invented, whatever case that was to be defended or thrown out, was now gone. The government was in the throes of changing. The Colonel was being deposed. A new leader, with a new army from the South, was now invading the North. They were freeing sympathetic border villages and committing acts of brutal violence against those not. The Colonel's brand new son born to a young wife, a baby boy, was placed into hiding with women in one of the camps. Hearing this, the new ruler ordered all male baby boys be killed there. Daughter, it is said this massacre of innocents happened, though it has never been confirmed.

I didn't know any of this at the time. No one did. And what do we really know now? The evidence is erased by a tide of blood, ever ebbing and flowing. The only witness to these nights of terror is the moon.

My daughter, as far as the world knew at that moment, the governing power was being democratically shifted from the previous ruling junta to the opposition party. An election had been held. Western observers had given a provisional green light: many voting irregularities, but an election nonetheless. Aid money would flow. The new leader appeared on television, waved, and made the peace sign, or the victory sign, just as his army was exacting revenge and crushing any residual resistance or loyalty to the former colonel who had gone into hiding.

During all this I lay prone in my cell. At some point I must have been found and determined to be alive. Were I a prisoner from the North, I would have met with a similar fate to some of the others around me, who were shot where they lay. Their bodies were dragged deep into the forest, stripped naked, and left for the cats or other animals to find and feed upon. But I was a foreigner. And they did not know who I was, or why I was there, only that they had been told I was a doctor. A foreign doctor. Captured by the previous government. Worth keeping alive, someone must have determined. Might be worth some money? Or, at least, some good will.

My daughter, wherever you are, if you read this, you must know that I confess to having given up. I lost the will to live. Can you forgive me? I was not heroic, or a freedom fighter. I was starving and semi-conscious and had given up.

=

PART THREE: PARIS & OENONE

And muffling up her comely head, and crying
"Husband!" she leapt upon the funeral pile,
And mixt herself with him and past in fire.

—Alfred, Lord Tennyson, "The Death of Oenone"

Paris

SHE MOISTENED MY LIPS, DABBING a cloth dampened with flat cola. With each pass of cloth, the wetness, the sugar, the shock of it pulled me from my inner state. And she sang so gently: songs of pain, of the earth and the trees, of the water and the mountains. How many days had she been singing? Some songs I think were meant for children, other songs that told stories of how this valley got its name, which animal represented this pond or another, songs to bring good harvests and plentiful fishing, songs of spirits that looked over and protected a sleeping village, songs of mother love and regeneration. Some songs called out and needed responses, and she sang these parts, my parts, for me.

I remember cola and melodies, her face close to mine, or my head on her lap or pulled to her breast. Her smell was raw earth and human. I was an injured animal and she built trust in minor increments, luring me out. Her face was open countryside, round and full, welcoming; it came into focus now and then. Her teeth were very white. Whenever I opened my eyes she smiled. I began to wish to make her smile, so I would try—with everything I had—to open my eyes. When I managed, she smiled again.

She began to give me spoonfuls of broth that had a warm, gamey, root vegetable taste. She washed my body down. The water evaporated off my skin—a forgotten sensation, downy arm hairs standing up with a wave of tingle. She caressed my earlobes. She sang and sang.

One day it rained and the air was heavy. She placed a wafer of unleavened bread on my tongue. My saliva came to life and I sucked on it until it dissolved. Come, this face seemed to say. Come back.

Some strength returned, and as it did, the presence of this woman would bring on unexpected waves of shame, or perhaps self-loathing. Now I would not die. Rather I would live with, and each day confront, my dismal decision to have simply given in. Was I too hard on myself? Were the brain chemicals that allowed me to peacefully shut down and prepare for death more potent than those that would now punish me for having submitted? I report only what occurred. I am my own witness, not my own doctor.

Her name is Oenone. She is a woman from the village that surrounds the jail. Originally, before the civil war, her people were from the very town where Helen and I were captured. She learned fair English from oil company workers. She does not know her age. These were the few answers she was able to whisper to me over the next few weeks. Or else I learned them later and have misplaced them further back in time.

There was a new guard. He would check on us now and again, knowing that I was showing signs of improvement. He was a strong, broad-shouldered man who did not smile. Each time he left she mocked him through gesture, in a sisterly kind of way—as if she knew him as a spindly boy, and could see right through his new-found authority. I could not yet tolerate my own weight so I had to roll over to relieve myself on the floor. She came daily, for an hour or two. She washed me, fed me. She sang and sang.

One day she instructed the guard to assist her. Together they held me upright and it was only then that I felt and properly understood the full weakness of my body. They held me there for only a few moments. The next day when she summoned the guard, again he came, and again they assisted me in standing up—for longer this time. Being made to stand recurred with each visit, along with the

171

washing and the feeding, the singing. How did she get the guard to do this, help with her instinctive physical therapy?

Eventually I began to stand unaided, each time for longer periods. Then I took a step or two, my feet dragging behind me across the floor. I ate more each day. I found I was able to sit upright by myself. Then I could stand unaided. I was putting on weight.

=====

Oenone

MY CHILD, WHEN I FIRST looked in upon this *blind* man, I was not sure he lived. But then a slight shiver, a shallow breath, a muscle twitch that occurred from some animal spirit of life, let me believe that he could be saved. Each rib pressed against the skin like a fallen animal on the plains and his eyes stared into his own vast night. I took his body and held it against my own. This is the first way, the beginning of how to return a person. As a mother holds a baby against her skin, I held this *blind* man and let him draw life back into his body from my own.

Then I began to give him songs. They were the ancient ones, telling of how the land was made, how the great serpent comes out of the sky and carves riverbeds and mountains with his body until it rains and rains and he leaves because he becomes so wet he cannot warm himself. The rainwater fills the rivers and many plants grow. Then fish and birds arrive, so happy to have found this beautiful place. But soon they fight over the best plants to eat, and one of the birds eats one of the fish and they never trust one another again.

Every time the rain stops the sun celebrates with a round circle of colours in the sky. Every colour has a place in the circle. The wild cats come down from the mountains and sing lovely songs in celebration of the circles of colours. A pack of wild dogs from another place are drawn to this singing. They come upon the cats and are so overwhelmed from the love they feel they try to capture the singing in their own mouths but in so doing they bite the cats' throats. The cats refuse to ever sing again so as to not make the dogs act in this way, and now they only purr and meow in ugly ways. The dogs have forevermore hated the cats for withholding their songs and so they hunt them, believing they can still make them sing. Having begun all this, the sun no longer tempts the cats, and only celebrates the end of the rain with half a circle of colours.

My child, these are the same ancient songs I've passed on to you. They are a part of this story. They are your story, they are part of everyone's story who is from this country, whether from the South or the North.

The story I tell is for you. I will give it over, from my lips to your small ears. I will tell it to you in the mornings as we eat fruit, and when as mother and daughter we wander down to the beach to collect smooth amber glass and seashell halves. I will sing it to you as you slip into sleep. I will tell it often, and in many different ways, until it becomes a part of you. This is the mother's way of telling stories. This way is more permanent than writing, which may be lost or sold, or burned by others. This way will make sure that the story is in you, lives as you live. If you choose, you may change it as you like. You may give it away. To your own daughter when she is ready, or else you might just want to hold it close and keep it alive but private. This story is for you.

In the last season of the war, we had journeyed here into the mountains to this village that overlooks the far coast. We were like the rolling, coloured pebbles on the beach after the tide has run out—suddenly here, suddenly exposed.

I first heard of him, of Paris, when the whispering began.

Oh, Mama Oenone, they would say. There is a forgotten *blind* man left in the jail!

You make this up. How could this be? I ask.

And they did not know. Just that it's true, they would protest.

Oh, child, these people were afraid. They had moved, and had been moved, all over the country, from a camp, to the city, to hideouts in the mountains. Mothers, sisters, fathers, or children were killed or lost to them. Their minds were not good— or so I thought. And they loved how these mouthfuls of gossip made their hearts beat faster and faster. They made up tales and told them to one another, and each time they grew in size. Their stories were dreams during the day; they were not about what they seemed. No, they were the night spirits overflowing, working their way out into the daylight any way they could.

You see, their pain was a swollen river. It broke its banks frequently. It had to. There was so much of it. Oh, Oenone, the army is coming. Oh, Oenone, there is a fire raging on the other side of the mountains and we shall all be burned alive. Oh, Oenone, there is a *blind* man being kept in the jail.

My child, you can see how they might not have been believed.

I had brought many of these people here, to this village. For many years before the war they followed my husband, and then me. In a camp outside the capital, I had schemed as I waited. How could my people return to our town? They wanted to know when; they wanted to have hope. I preached patience. Those who believed followed me on our long journey when the time finally came. They stayed close to me for all that time out of loyalty, out of love, out of faith that when our moment arrived, we could return and make the past present once more.

Others just arrived here in this village and we met for the first time. They had nowhere else to turn and just followed along. Still others arrived back here because this is where they are originally from. I know them from long ago, or knew their parents.

==

Paris

THIS IS FOR YOU, DOCTOR Paris, Oenone said, holding
out her hand and dropping a small tooth into my
palm. This belonged to my son.

I thanked her for the tooth, without yet
knowing its significance; I did understand it to be an
important gift she was giving me. I carefully tucked
it in a crack in one of the walls. I knew each gap
now as intimately as the lifelines on my palm, the
scars on my body.

I came to understand later, from Oenone as
well as from others in the village, that her son was
four years old when he died. A snake came and
took him from her in the night. I imagine it was a
viper. The custom is that a tooth is removed from
the body and given to the grieving family—the
dead not needing to eat in the spirit world. It is
the ultimate gift, a physical remembrance of a

dead loved one, in this place without easy access to photographs or film.

To the spirit world went her son, from it I came to her. An unfair trade but one she accepted with total commitment and love from the first.

I had been saved despite myself.

=

Oenone

THIS IS MY ANCESTRAL VILLAGE. I lived here in these mountains until I was girl who began her bleeding. Then I was married and left with my husband for the town. He was charming. He could fix engines. As a young man he had plans. I was so in love with him it made me frightened with worry. He and I were in love as infants. We played together in the mountains surrounding this village. We found water holes, explored, trapped animals, collected plants. As we grew, it was assumed that we would always be together. I always understood that he would be the one I would marry, like we had pretended as children. So, when it happened just the way I had always expected, I felt lucky.

He had already begun to change, even as we grew hair on our bodies, even as we learned what men and women do with one another. He was jealous and would thrash out at me if he suspected I had spoken to another boy in the village. His temper worsened and after we were married, when he announced that we would be going to the town so he could start a mechanical business and become rich, I agreed partly out of adventure, but also out of fear. What would he do to me if I said no? Could I even say no?

For a while in the town our life was very interesting. His business kept him very busy. He befriended many men, far and wide, and they admired his confidence and his easy way of doing business. We made money by doing business with the oil company. Legitimate business. He taxied their people to and from the capital. He fixed their jeeps and trucks. I also worked with them as a servant, looking after their children. I learned how to speak to the women, the wives of the men who ran the oil company.

When he announced that he was going to run for political office, I was pleased. His temper remained fierce and I thought that the scrutiny of public office would make him more cautious. It had the opposite effect. He grew arrogant and violent. Hitting me across the face, burning me with a cigarette end, accusing me of being the lover of one of the *blind* oil company men. I did not even know who he was speaking about.

By this time I had given birth to a baby boy. With the child still feeding from my breast, I came across some papers in his mechanic's garage that were plainly letters agreeing to services my husband would provide the oil company. They were unsigned on white paper and described how he would be given money and weapons to enlist men to help him protect the building of a pipeline.

I trembled as I read.

These letters, addressed to him as the regional member of government, boldly outlined my husband's criminal activity, the bribes and profiteering, in such basic terms that anyone could understand. He was, obviously, afraid of no one. He believed he was unstoppable.

The following Sunday he was due to speak to a group of town elders about government issues, but he asked me to cancel it as he had to go to the capital. I agreed, but I did not cancel it. Instead, I attended. I brought with me the letters and I addressed the group directly and without fear. There were a number of very good men in this gathering, including a religious man, the honest police inspector, and the editor of the newspaper. I read the letters. I announced I needed protection from my husband, that I was, as of this moment, no longer married to him.

The entire town knew what had happened before he arrived back. I had gone into hiding, my dear friends providing for me in a room in the Colonial Hotel. The army came from the capital to maintain peace. He was thrown from office and before he was arrested he fled the town for the North. My heart heavy, I hoped to never see him again.

The next election was sprung upon us due to the rising discontent in the North. I was pressed into running for office, the town desiring an end to oil company corruption. With my boy just one year old, I became the leader of the region—a position I held until the war broke out, until we abandoned the town for the capital, and then after it became unsafe, we were forced into the camps.

Many of us from the camp stayed together. We waited out the war in the camp but it was a mean existence. Chaos, disease, disappearances. Controlled by the northern army, we could not return to the town; it was not safe; the time was not right. So, my idea grew, which was to escape the camp and head for this village. I made my case to those in my care. I spoke out one night in the camp. We stood, a collection of the lost and forgotten, around a fire lit in a drum, the women feeding babies and children playing at our feet in the dirt. Satellites tracked across the open night sky and an impatient truck horn sounded on and off, reaching us across the vast camp, interrupting the dreams of dogs feasting in their sleep.

I know the way through the mountains, I said. I know where to escape if danger arrives. I know where there is a water spring between two rocks, where our boys can hunt small animals and birds. I know the way. If you have the strength, if you have in your hearts the love and trust for one another, we can go there together. We can wait there in secret, quietly, for the tide to change, for war to end, for the South to regain control, for liberation, for salvation, for peace.

The walk was long and hard. We followed the dry riverbed though the southern mountains. After we finished the food we brought, we ate some berries and found water often enough, or we dug for it. Across the plains we were in full view and we travelled at night.

The dangers were many. We woke to screaming. It was almost at dawn. A panther was upon us, still as death, waiting in the shadows. Huddled, we quietened down the one among us who had woken us in fright. We breathed as one. The minutes ticked by. The cat was still, ready to spring. Ready to take one of our children. Where were her hungry cubs? We waited. The sky was lightening by the minute. Long orange and pink streaks of sun rubbed against the horizon behind the cat. Crickets started up. We waited. I thought of my former husband. How he waited for the right time to pounce on our town,

take over by force that which he could not by love. I
saw him that morning when I went to the Colonial
Hotel to help out my dear friends. I saw him pretending to sell leather. I did not know he was
waiting to attack and capture foreigners for ransom.
His handsome smile drew people to him. Although
short, he looked and talked like the kind of man
who is substantial. But he hides his real self and,
although he smiles, he thinks many other things. He
plots how he can charm you with his smile and then
he uses you. He stood there selling leather for three
days. Everyone in our town seeing him there, not
speaking to him out of disgust, just waiting for him
to leave or for me to throw him out of the town. But
I would not speak to him! My pride said ignore him.
He knew me, predicted I would do this. And from
his leather stand, unopposed, unarmed, he orches-
trated the invasion from the middle of our town.

I stood and walked toward the cat. I clapped
my hands loudly. Go! I said. Leave and go.

———

Paris

WHAT WAS IN THE AIR? My daughter, I woke more fully, more definitively than I had in months. Low thrumming sounds drifted in and out of the cell, through the walls themselves, through the hole near the ceiling. She had been coming every day, having coaxed me back from death. There is no other way to describe her treatment. It was a gentle and persistent lure. The songs and food, her touch and smell, reached into the murk of my consciousness, of my decision to surrender, and argued for a stay. Once she had a toehold, she'd pressed the issue. She sang and sang, she fed, and somehow I was not gone yet. An idea of me still existed and was brought back to lead the rest of me out of oblivion.

Where was she that day? Now I could sit on my own, now I could stand with some help and take several steps. I was eager to impress her. Each stutter of a step I took gave her pleasure and I wanted to perform this act again now. I was ready for her, but she did not come. Instead, as I lay on the floor with my head resting on my arm, I could feel the sound in the earth, entering through every surface, molecules vibrating with a new energy.

Was she safe? Suddenly I became frightened for her. I called out for the guard, something I had never done before. I called the one who had been helping me stand, who took his orders not from his commander, but from Oenone. Hold his arm. Now lift. Set him down. Be sure to catch him if he falls. These were the instructions, some of which I understood by their context, others because I knew some words. And she would give me snatches of instruction in English too. Put weight on your foot now. Press up. That's enough for today.

No guard came. I listened harder at the door. Called again, this time much weaker. I did not know if there were other prisoners still in the jail. I had always been aware of life on the other side of my walls. It is something you just begin to feel, my daughter. But I did not have the sensation that there was a man, any men—angry, hurt, hungry, masturbating, or insane—close by now. Why am I alone in the jail? I was healthier than I had been in months. My mind was clear and working in full. So I waited. I lay on the ground and waited for Oenone, feeling for the vibrations, reading the change that moved in the air. Whatever the change was, it was connected to her absence. I was sure of that. She would come. She would come because I needed her to, because I believed, suddenly, my face against the dirt, that she needed me too and that by saving my life in the manner she had, she was bound to me.

The vibrations of the ground became louder.

How had she saved my life? She did not know my heart rate or blood pressure. She was not monitoring my breathing. She inserted no IV line to give antibiotics or fluids or nutrients. I had starved. I was shutting down. My fat reserves had been completely exhausted with only protein as a fuel source for my body. Organ function must have declined. How many times have I treated people in this state? Was I septic? Had Oenone not saved me, what would have been my ultimate cause of death? Cardiac arrest brought on by tissue degradation and electrolyte imbalance?

=====

Oenone

I LED THE WOMEN AND children onward and we reached the far mountains without many deaths. Most of the young ones made it alive, though not all. Pyres were needed along the way, tears fell to the ground as the cinders drifted skyward.

On the way to the mountain village, we passed the town. At night a few of us crept along its empty streets. Starving dogs and cats were about. The soldiers' camp was on the far side of the slums. The main street was quiet and I snuck into my home. The walls were the same; some pieces of broken furniture were still about, but nothing else. In my husband's garage everything was taken.

We crept inside the Colonial Hotel. In the basement, there was a locked door. Black and hard to see at all, my hand reached up along the top of the wall for the crack in the ledge. Yes, there it was, my fingers had it, the key.

Inside the pantry were still some tins of tomatoes, some olives, sardines. Dusty bottles of Fanta and cola. We carried what we could, and the next night went back for the rest. Everything was shared. The children's faces—confused, delighted, eating this *blind* food, having had so little to eat— this was enough to keep us going. Some became sick with diarrhea because the food was too strong. For me, the salt of the olives, the oily sardines, the fizz of the Fanta and cola—I had tried these many times before the war, but they did not taste as good as they now did.

Oh yes, my child, the key. After my husband went away, I often helped in the kitchen there. The owners were my close friends, a foreign couple who came to our town to visit but stayed on to renovate and run the hotel.

I knew where the key was because it was right where I'd left it. I was in the basement of the hotel the morning the war arrived, angry that my former husband was still across the road pretending to sell leather. I thought he was there because of me, that he was taunting me.

The pantry had a strong metal door. Maybe no one had managed to break it open? So we went to see. Inside we found that only mice had entered.

They had long since taken the flour and other grains. The cans were right where I'd unloaded them all those years earlier.

So my child, it was with full bellies and smiles that we pressed onward for the mountains. They were steeper and we could not take the main trails and roads for fear of the soldiers. When we finally came upon the village it was morning. Something was wrong. I had expected that all of the huts and buildings would be fallen or burned, which they were. But I did not expect to see a northern army building. It had a metal roof with cinderblock walls. Truck after truck must have brought these materials here. Why? We stayed away a good distance in the bush. The children were taken farther up the mountain where their crying or playing would not be heard.

It was a jail. There seemed to be two or three guards only; young recruits who sat around playing cards and sleeping mostly. They had a fire where they cooked food, and sometimes went inside to check on or feed the prisoners.

Mama Oenone, oh what are we going to do? the people asked of me.

I could not show them my concern at the presence of the jail, or that I did not know what the right course of action was to take. So I stood up and walked toward where the huts and buildings were. Several were in some state of repair and just needed their walls supported. I began to fix up one of these huts. I did not acknowledge the men, who I could feel looking at me. I just went about my work. In twos and threes, the other women came out of the bush to help me. We fixed two of the huts and spent the night inside. I'm not sure any of us slept. But the morning came and we still had our arms and legs, so we set to work on one of the buildings that needed just a roof. It took much of the day, but by nightfall it was ready. We sent for the children and the other women. This became the pattern of our days, finding food in the bush, getting water, feeding children, fixing huts and the other buildings that we could.

The northern soldiers ignored us. We began to understand that they were especially young; a commander came by jeep every few days to inspect the jail. We would hide in the bush when we heard the motor on its way up the mountain. It was late in the day of their rule, and they knew it. Why bother with stray women and children? We watched the boy guards though, especially at night.

There was an incident early on that I will tell you about, my child. There are parts of this story that are hard to pass along. Sometimes I think it might be better if you didn't have such a complete story. But if the story is given properly it must be intact and whole.

There was drinking at the jail after dark one evening, rough laughing. Two guards came upon one of our huts, a machete drawn. One held down a girl who was not yet properly a woman, the other stood with the knife held high. I could see and smell he was drunk. While the girl still struggled and pleaded with the boy who was now on top of her, from behind I came upon the one with the knife, smashing a rock against his skull. He fell to the ground. With his long knife now in my hand, the other boy stopped his struggle and stood, his eyes frightened.

Mama, I am a good boy. He pointed at the one on the ground who now had blood in his hair. He tells me it is time for me to know a woman, that's all. I don't come here again.

I took the machete tip and dug it into him. I curse you, I say looking at his eyes. If you ever again try to take from a woman what is not being freely given, you will die every time you sleep. I will come to you in every dream and run this blade across your throat. This curse cannot be lifted. Take this man away and throw his body from a mountainside so they do not think you are responsible for his death. Tell them he became drunk and mad and ran away into the bush.

Some days later the boy was joined by a new guard, but none ever came to our huts again when we slept.

We waited. Word of the change in power came with snatches of story brought to us by fleeing women and children. They'd been told where we were headed and had set out on their own journey to find us, in desperation. Were there others that did not make it, did not find us?

One woman arrived in our village to tell us that elections were being held in the capital, and that she had witnessed *blind* troops in large trucks with weapons on the streets. She said that the northern army had retreated to the other side of the southern mountains. Men and women came and filmed this change in power, she said, for worldwide news. The people gave fish and flowers to the *blind* troops as gifts, urging them to stay. But she had no further information on the outcome of the election. She had left on a truck before voting day. She had to find her husband, she said. Later, she said, she found herself lost on the road, hungry, and followed other women into the mountains, hoping together they would find us.

Increasingly, newcomers travelled the road over the mountains and found us, bringing stories of the new peace, the election victory of the South. A landslide, they said. There had been music in the streets, offered one. Shops opened and the first train ran in four years, said another.

Then our village became a battlefield. Northern troops arrived in trucks and jeeps to evacuate the jail. We fled into the bush, taking the children with us, high into the mountains. I stayed nearby, hidden. The men were tearing down their barracks, evacuating prisoners, when southern troops appeared on the opposite road and a firefight broke out. The northern soldiers were greater in number and they lit fires and shot and shot, setting the bush and a number of our huts ablaze and upending cans of petrol as they fled. Through the smoke and shouting I watched as the northern jeeps drove off, around the mountain, in retreat.

We came down out of the mountains as the sun was setting. Three southern soldiers remained behind at the jail; the others pressed on after the northern army. I went over to speak with them. One of the men was the son of a woman I knew well from the town. She was married to a crooked dentist—well, not so much a dentist as a man who pulled out people's teeth for too much money. My child, this is funny, as a boy the dentist's son had a perfect smile. All his teeth, right there in place. And he carried it along with him into manhood. Yes, he was handsome.

Mama Oenone, we captured a northern soldier and have found several prisoners, he said to me after we recognized one another. One is almost dead.

Can he be saved? I asked.

He is a *blind*. We want to save him. He might be worth money to a foreign government. Can you help? We are too busy with the other prisoners.

Not if he is to be sold, I said.

My mother always told me you were the most principled politician she'd known.

Did your mother vote for me? I would have thought that impossible. Your father hated me, but loved my husband.

My mother loved you. You were the opposite of my father, whom she loathed. We laughed together at the memory of the crooked dentist.

I will save the *blind* man. But I have a whole village here to look after. Nothing more.

That is all we ask, he said. We do not know who any of the other prisoners are anyway. They speak about places that no longer exist and factions none of us know. We will hold them until further orders.

The next morning we awoke to a scuffle. The northern soldier was screaming and crying. It was the guard. The boy I had cursed. The son of the dentist was pointing a rifle into his back and asking him the real name of the Colonel. The boy did not know. He was pushed to his knees.

The dentist's son then said, to the sky more than anything else, The Colonel killed my father.

You follow the Colonel. So I kill you. And the shot rang out and hung in the air before being taken in by the trees and the clouds and the soil. The boy had been shot in the head, the barrel of the gun having been pushed into his mouth.

My child, this is the horror of war. There is no innocent, no guilty, no law, only individual men who have had their stories taken, and so are no longer men at all.

I saved two bottles of cola from the Colonial Hotel. I thought that they should be kept in case we needed them to bargain with northern soldiers, or even southern soldiers. What situations would we find ourselves in? So I kept two. I decided to open one to use on the *blind* prisoner.

The dentist's son helped me lift the *blind* prisoner to his feet. We did this several times a day. He began to talk English. His name was Paris. He was a doctor.

In the village we cooked in a drum left over from the northern army. We made soups from the old bush recipes that our mothers taught us as girls. We laughed together as some among us remembered our mothers cooking here in this village. Then, when we left here we believed we would never return, never eat this food again! But here we are. We laughed together as we chopped roots and wild herbs, skinned and cleaned rodents and song birds, stoked the fire.

I fed him the soup. He talked now in broken thoughts. With effort his spoken language came back to my tongue. I still remembered many of the words. But how to say the ideas I needed for he and I to understand one another? It was not always simple. We strained to overcome.

What crime did this man commit? My child, I had to know. The dentist's son did not know. How could he? The prisoners were simply transferred from the North to the South when the jail changed hands. So when he was strong enough, after I had sung to him for many nights and days, fed him and rocked him, walked him and cleaned his body with water and soap given to me by the guard, after I had done all this, I held him close in the early evening and asked him to confess his crime.

My child, this is what he said: *I gave up on myself.* Oh there was such shame in his voice, and on his face.

Now I was shy. I had already had the stirrings, you see, the great rush from within, my steps hurrying when I was to next go to him, bring him food, caress his face, sing to him. I had already felt these intimate signs. Each alone not enough to notice, but when gathered up and braided together around and around, a vessel was being made. Something to hold in the palms, like a cup. Then bigger, in outstretched hands, a bowl. Then larger still. Until you needed your arms open wide just to carry its breadth and depth, a barrel. I was in love with the *blind* doctor, Paris.

When I lost my son in the dark of the mountains to the snake, but before I threw his lifeless, innocent body on the pyre and poured myself into the sky until I felt no more, felt nothing left of him, I took a tooth. I have kept it in the fold of my dress, next to me, ever since. There is always more left. It can never be all poured away. There is a private place that a mother keeps something of her dead child. A place she can go when there is time, when it is safe and when she can be alone. There, she may hold what is left and she may be for a while the mother again of that child. She may bring that child back to life, hear his delightful laugh, his curious questions, feel the breath of him against her cheek and neck. She may return the purity of him to this world, and share her love with the child at night, even when in a camp as the rest of the women and children sleep, or on the long march across the plain under the stars, or in a mountain hut waiting for a war to turn.

Now I had a new innocent. My son had given me a *blind* doctor. I gave Paris the small tooth. I used the words in his language to explain this gift. Did he understand?

As his strength returned he changed from a prisoner to my lover. He learned that all loves are one in this country. As the rain falls into the sea, as the dead animal seeps into the ground or is eaten, as fire makes way for tiny green shoots, so love once shared and accepted becomes all the other loves that came before.

My child is my husband, they are both my parents, my son is Paris. You are me.

This is a part of the story that you must grow to understand, my child. This is our country's way to make the past the future again. It is our song. So if I do not tell it well enough, or if you do not hear it again and again, something may happen in your life that will take your story from you. War can do this. The death of your child can do this. This story will keep your basket tightly woven and you strong.

When Paris took the tooth I watched him look it over. He rolled it between the thumb and finger of those white hands. Then he tucked it into a crack in the wall. Safe there, he said. Then I washed his limp, failing body with water and some soap. I spooned soup into his mouth. I sang to him all the songs he would need for his story to begin again. After many days of attending to him, I opened the cell door and found him sitting upright by himself. He smiled. In his palm he held the tooth. Together we sang.

═══

Paris

THERE WAS MUSIC. FINE BUT broken threads of song were finding their way to me. The bright sound of metal on metal, an improvised drum, kept the rhythm. Other hard woods were being struck together in a tapping that counterpointed the deeper tin sound. The voices, women's voices, rose and fell away in call and response, infused with celebratory joy and cries of change, of worship, of faith, and of luck. It all washed against my cell in a high tide. They did not let up, but continued on for the day, ebbing and flowing, as different villagers took the lead.

At times their voices were strong and clear, other times the procession or gathering moved away and I lost the structure of it as it untangled into threads of sound again. As the day deepened and night approached, I heard children crying amidst

the singing. I smelled the sweet smoke of a bon-
fire roasting meat and of something similar to can-
nabis. All day, coming and going, were trucks or
jeeps. Greetings of welcome, horns sounding to say
hello or goodbye, and a handbell was introduced
into the music following the arrival of one of the
motorcades.

At night, guns fired into the air in rapid suc-
cession. Cries of joy and more song erupted. There
was alcohol in the laughter now, a frenzy that was
not present earlier. I collapsed in exhaustion from
my second-hand exposure to this revelry, of the
quality of sweet pain it unleashed in me, a sensation
that was so distant I'd have thought it unrecoverable,
like freedom itself.

═

Oenone

IN THE MORNING I WENT to him. Many of the children in the village were already awake, wandering around, their mothers still asleep. A truck's worth of soldiers that were passing through had spent the night on the ground under the trees by the jail. They remained asleep as I passed them. The dentist's boy had left in the night so there were no guards as I entered the wire gate to the jail. The keys to the padlocks hung on the nails in the painted white board, with numbers on them. Yesterday, there were four prisoners remaining. I saw that all the doors were open except Paris's. The dentist's son had left him for me.

I took the key from the white board and walked down the dirt corridor between the twenty cells. His was second from the end. I opened his door.

Paris sat with his back against the wall. He

was smiling already, having heard the lock being opened. He knew it was me. He held out his hand. In it was my son's baby tooth. We had elections, I told him. All night the soldiers have been passing through the mountains. We have been celebrating. The junta is gone. Our soldiers tell us that the northerners ran away across the far hills, back into their territory. They ran across the old border— like children in trouble.

Come, I said to him.

Paris leaned his weight against me and took tentative steps toward the cell door. At its threshold, he stopped.

There are no more guards, no more war. Come, I said to him again. You are free.

All across the village the women were waking, tired from the singing, drumming, and dancing that went on until the moon disappeared behind the mountain. Many of them no longer have husbands. Many just have children, or grandchildren. The soldiers were also awake. They were cleaning their rifles, packing up their equipment, preparing to descend the mountains. Last night, as the trucks and jeeps came and went, some men said to us that they intended to continue with the army. Others were enthusiastic about training with the new force of police being established by *blind* soldiers from foreign countries down in the capital. Still others said simply that they would put down guns altogether, go back to their villages, plant crops, or re-establish their businesses from a decade ago. Carrying on like nothing had transpired. Those men just shrugged, *What else is a man supposed to do*? And they were right in a way. Getting back to normal life has to start with at least a few people acting that way.

Some men knew where their wives or girl-friends were; others did not and feared the worst. But it had been a night of hope, not fear. We had won an aspect of the war; the past could return now.

Step by slow step, Paris and I emerged from the prison. The business of the village came to a stop as they saw me assisting a gaunt *blind* man with a long beard. Each step was agony for Paris. He shielded his eyes from the light and colours—I was not sure he could see properly. These steps were the first ones he had taken beyond the walls of his cell in many seasons. The children approached us first.

Mama Oenone, they asked, where did you find this *blind* old man?

And in our language, as clear as if he'd spoken it his entire life, he answered them: Dead in the ground.

Paris

MY DAUGHTER, THE FIRST DAYS of freedom were a dream. From isolation, and because my eyesight was so poor, I had seen so few faces in the past years. I had forgotten how interesting they were. I drew them close, one after another, and saw them smiling or frowning. I watched as they went about living. Putting food into their mouths, or bathing, or shaking their heads at this flavour or that smell. They petted dogs and cooed at babies. Oh, babies—the total innocence and helplessness of them as they fed at a mother's breast. I held one in my arms, putting the foot in the palm of my hand, feeling its reflexive strength, the smooth vulnerability of its tendon.

Oenone stayed close beside me. Always with food, always asking me to move. Get up and walk, she would insist. And I knew she was right. To keep moving was the thing to do, but the onslaught of these new sensations, my fatigue, made it difficult. Still, she insisted and I gave in, climbing to my feet every few hours, eventually walking from one end of the village to the other.

For the first few days I was a curiosity. The children especially wanted to talk to me. They asked me how I knew some of their language. And I told them about the other prisoners in the jail who taught me words over the years. Then, after a while, with so much else that was new and undergoing change in the village, the interest in me moved on. Soldiers came and went. A few men who had once lived in the village returned and began to rebuild huts and buildings. Other men came and reunited with wives and children. Some stayed, opting for the shelter of this village as the country re-established itself. Others left for their ancestral lands and towns.

One man entered the village slowly. During the elections, he had escaped from a prison camp in the night and walked from the northern part of the country here. I heard his voice before I saw his face.

Doctor Paris. My brother! So we both live, Hector said, coming toward me. It was the *ghost* soldier. We embraced for the first time. He was well and fit. Unlike me, he had been fed and had been made to work building roads and fences.

Where will you go now? I asked him.

I have no plans. I have no wife. My sister, my

mother, where are they? Should I walk the country in search of them, another *ghost* on the road serving out a new sentence? That is not freedom, man. I do not believe it. I just wanted to come here, to see if I could find word of you. Once I'd done that, I suppose I was going to go to the town, or maybe to the capital. Catch some fish and sell them. No more politics though. Ah brother, he said, I don't know who I am anymore.

Oenone put my brother Hector to work in the village. She ordered him about with the same affection that she did everyone. He was strong and intelligent. After some months Hector took a wife, a kind woman with two children and no husband to help her. They built a mud-walled house with a metal roof that my brother carried on his back through the mountains from the market in the town. But I am skipping ahead.

One of the soldiers had scissors. Oenone cut my hair short, and trimmed my beard. She picked the lice from my body. When I could walk unaided, after I'd begun to put on weight and could help with light work in the village, a community she was now the leader of and managed with a series of nods and waves of the hand, she came to me with a cloth draped over something.

What is it? I was sitting in the shade of a tree after a midday meal.

A present, she said. I asked Hector to get it. It is for you, from me.

I pulled back the cloth from her outstretched arms. It was an English language newspaper. Published in the capital only last week, she said. I pulled it to my face slowly and smelled the paper and ink. My eyes were closed. I kept them closed.

Do you read English? I asked her.

Only a little. Directions. Food. Numbers, she said.

I handed the newspaper back to her, and asked, What does the date say?

And she told me. And I nodded, first figuring the distance between the time on the newspaper from the café and now. Then I calculated my age.

You don't want it, she asked.

I don't think so, I said.

Later that evening Oenone came to me and took me by the hand. She led me along a winding path, through rock walls, and down and down until we came to a pool of water. In silence, she undressed me and then herself. Together we entered the spring water, step by step until we plunged in together no longer touching the bottom. I was swimming, the feeling of a miracle itself, strokes done by memory from childhood, to keep my head above the water. There was only starlight and I could see nothing but shadows and light, the reflected brightness of Oenone's eyes and teeth, which I kept close as we became lovers on a smooth ledge, in that echoey chamber of rocks with the heavy air so needed by ferns and moss.

I had been held as a prisoner of war for no reason at all. My incarceration was precipitated by no act of my own, no crime. I was never used as ransom, never traded in exchange for other prisoners held by the other side. I was never rescued by my own government. In that pool with Oenone, clean and alive, I was overcome with gratitude. She was the first human in so long who had been moved to act selflessly, with my interests in mind. While I remained a man with the courage to reject faith, was I to be given no answers, no insight, nothing to explain my lot, except circumstance, chance, or misfortune? Then Oenone pulled my face to hers. The water upturned the night sky and she smiled broadly. Here was my answer to why, right before me.

Oenone

I LEFT THE VILLAGE ON a donkey ride into town where I'd heard *blind* doctors had a hospital tent and cured people. I did not tell Paris. I knew our mountain village was his home. I was to be his wife. Arrangements were being made for a celebration.

Paris *had* recovered, but there was a different sickness growing in him, something else. I could feel it. He must not become sick again. I made him eat the root of the tree that heals. But I also went to foreign doctors for their medicine too.

Their tents were white with strong ropes. They moved quickly and spoke in languages I did not understand. They began to examine me. No, I am not sick, I explained. It is my husband back in our village. Yes, I used the word husband early, to help along the seriousness. I spoke the name of what I believed was wrong with Paris, in English.

212

They nodded and talked among themselves. They explained that I was to bring him for them to examine. They refused to give me medicine to take to him. I did not tell them who Paris was, that he would know what to do with the medicine.

It was up to me, to the ancient ways.

When I returned, Paris did not ask where I went for those two days, but instead he left for a short while to help a number of the women gather the fruit that was ripe on the trees in the next valley. They returned and we peeled and ate the fruit all evening, the juice running down the children's faces through the dust on their cheeks.

Paris began to go with Hector to fish and hunt for crabs on the other side of the mountains on the coast. It is a long journey, several hours there and back, and it was heavy for him to share in carrying the baskets of crab up the mountain to our village. But he insisted on going, on sharing in the work with Hector. He was stronger now, but I could see in his eyes, feel on the surface of his skin, that the sickness was spreading deep within him.

On the night of the wedding, the youngest girls made chains of purple flowers and put them in my hair. Everyone sang and danced around the fire. Paris and I were seated beside one another under a tree, as is the custom. He knew more and more of our words by then and played with the children so they could teach new ones to him. He no longer wished for me to speak to him in English.

He asked Hector to find him a stack of clean paper and a writing pen in the town on his last trip there. My child, Paris began to write every evening. He holds the pages close to his face so he can see his way across the lines. At the beginning he seemed unsure of how to do it, to write words, but he pushed himself every night and page after page became filled with his words crossing them. He kept them in a neat pile in our house, in his room. He told me he was writing to someone, telling a long story so it was no longer trapped inside him.

It was the sickness that made him write. He still did not know of its presence. I grated the amber root and put it in his soup. He believed I was continuing to nurse him back to life from the prison cell. I made him suck the darkest leaves of the shade bush, the one with the white flowers in the spring. He wrote and wrote. We did not talk about it further.

===

Paris

MY DAUGHTER, LIFE IN THIS village moves in purposeful waves that I quickly become used to and understand. We collect water each day. We pick fruit, find plants, herbs, and roots in the mornings. Other days I trek with my brother down the mountain pathways to the coast and catch crabs on the rocks, throw a net out into the surf to catch feeding fish. We lie in wait at the water holes for thirsty wild boars or other animals to shoot.

Oenone and I are married.

Many in the village are doing this, stabilizing life for the children. The people treat me warmly. I am not strong, but I go with my brother or the other men fishing or hunting so we have items to sell in the town's market.

I do not leave the village's world. Aid workers are now established in the town. There are rations being flown in to ensure there is enough food in the regions outside the capital before the first harvest can be reaped. There is a field hospital, the very kind I once worked at.

The villagers dismantled the jail for materials. They left the main building standing and we used several of the locked cells to store grain or other supplies that are occasionally brought in by truck or jeep. Oenone and I manage the old jail for the village and guard the supplies. We charge a modest storage fee. We use the money to buy food and tools. We live in a hut adjoining the end of the jail. We are the former jail's caretakers because, for many nights following my release, I was inconsolable. I became delirious and anxious. Finally, I did fall asleep. Oenone found me the next morning. I had wandered into the jail, back into my cell where I had crawled onto the floor, as I had done for so many years, and fell deeply asleep. I found I had to continue to sleep there. So my brother and I punched a hole in the outer wall and mudded in a doorway, and we built a hut against the jail wall. Oenone and I have lived there since. We sleep together in my cell. It is our bedroom.

Something new is wrong with me. I was gaining weight easily then it began to fall away. Lately I have had nausea in the evenings. I have a pain in my abdomen that comes and goes, and last night it radiated to my back. My stools are pale. I know she suspects there is a new sickness inside me. Her healing instincts are profound. We cannot face a new threat. We choose not talk about it. She wants me to live. She has work to do here, and she wants me by her side. Oenone went into the town alone. I know she saw the physicians there. Of course, even if they understood her, what prescription could they offer?

My daughter, why am I still here? Why do I not take Oenone to the town, contact the embassy, be found, saved and if not healed, at least tell my story, and briefly rejoin the world? I know this is cancer. I am far, far along. By the time I recognized it, paid attention to it with the last wisps of my medical memory, it was too late for choices. My body is echoing my father's.

Why am I still here? The answer is simple and complex. Simple, in that I may finally do whatever I wish. Complex, in that she loves me with the force of a great shame. She understands I have given my life over to her and her country; and that her former husband was a traitor. She is a leader. She loves her country and these people. But she is shamed at the inhumanity of the war—that she is connected to people, especially one man, that would have perpetrated it, that she was unable to prevent it beginning or stop it after it had begun. I am impossibly drawn to her honour and devotion.

Are she and Helen so different? For all I know Helen is right back in the town, not a day away from here, saving lives. But no, I believe she is looking after you, my daughter. She has made the choice of motherhood; it is the only choice. I became a memory, a turning point in time. Does she think of me now? Maybe. Maybe not. In the end, if we are each able to find home in some way, a connection to place and country and another person who would die for you and for whom you would die, then that is more than can be hoped for from life.

I am simply Paris. I work as a caretaker of a building. I feed my family, and I love and am loved by a strong, beautiful woman. I often break bread with a brother. I survived a war. I belong here because I am accepted here. Simple. And complex. Crab. Pear fruit. Marriage. Oenone gives me her body as an apology. Weekly, a truck goes with our meat, or fruit, or wild harvest bound for the town's market. In the night sky the outlines of clouds roam free over the mountains, but they do not send me to sleep. I need a room with no windows. I desire the certainty of solitude, the answers brought by captivity. The truck, it just comes and goes; I do not get on it.

Unless she can save me for a second time, we understand I am again choosing to die in my cell.

I cannot explain my decision other than, as I reach the end of this writing, it is different than before. Oenone saved me, showed me life as I had never understood it, all so I might write it down, pass on to you the story of my life, your history.

My daughter, I often dreamed of Helen's swollen belly floating in the sea, the wind pushing it like a sail. She runs aground on an island and takes you from inside herself, washing you in the sea, pulling you to her breast. I am not on the island, but I can always see the two of you there. You are safe.

Oenone is pregnant. As I continue to lose weight and strength, hers seems to increase. This village has lost its middle from diseases, war, hunger, droughts, and floods. We are mostly old and children, the beginning and the end. The centre of the story was largely torn out. It continues this way unless war does not return, unless this child chooses to stay here and insists on building upon these new beginnings.

One day strong, young foreigners come walking through the middle of the village. Suddenly, there are four white people before me. I have no time to retreat, or perhaps hide. They are travelling, hiking the country on foot. That is all of their business. These mountains are so beautiful, they say. They talk about themselves. They do not ask me who I am, or why I am here. I say only I have been here a long time. From before the war? they ask. Yes, I say. But what this *really* means—doesn't actually mean much of anything to them. So I offer them food at our hut. They want to know how to get to the coast, and ask can they camp there easily enough, or should they be worried about wild cats or panthers? They leave with smiles and easy laughter, which brings unexpected brightness to me.

The entire world has moved on from the war. Now foreign young people—with money for bribes and the stomach for adventure—can walk this country and be worried only about wild cats and poor infrastructure.

They leave a *Lonely Planet* book for me as a gift. It is about this county, my country, they are passing through. They no longer need it. They've seen it all, they say. Tentatively at first, then eagerly, I read it cover to cover and learn about my adopted home through my old eyes. It is all lies. Or else, it is the colourful, happy gaps around the truth. From ten years of civil war comes a single paragraph mentioning generals, *coups d'état*, governments that came and went. The village is not on the map, but the larger town is, and is presented with some photographs as "a must-see." I read about the Colonial Hotel—*it has the best pastries and coffee in the plains region. Plan to stay several nights. Take a hike through the nearby mountain foothills.*

You are half a sister. Our daughter has the name for *River*. She came forth into the world quickly in a single push and gush. I caught River in my hands, wiping her clean, separating her from Oenone, and then handing her back to her mother. As she nursed I heard Oenone sing a song to her that I remember from my first days of recovery in the cell. They bury the placenta here.

Eyes and ears and mouth and nose, is what I sing to her, knowing that's not the beginning, but that it's all I can recall my own father singing. I see my father's eyes in River, and I see my eyes. Are they your eyes too?

My daughter, here is the end of what I write. Here is all I have to give you. Once I had nothing but time, and now I have almost none left. I hold the baby with arms that are weak. Oenone feeds both the baby and me, one after another. I shrink under the helpless curse of this disease, the originating site of which I will never know. I am withering so quickly. It is my time now. There are no gods to intervene and deflect this arrow. The last truck has left the village. Oenone did not look up at it, did not look at me with hopeful eyes that I might ask to be put upon it, that I might wish to live and see this baby that I now hold grow into a child, then a young woman, then a mother herself.

I have written all there is; this is my course, to die in Oenone's arms. I will be a father to River in the way I have been to you. As I have already been with you the entire time, so will I be with her. So, I ask you: share this story with your sister. Read the words to River. Tell her I mean them, my fatherly love, for her too, in equal measure.

And, Helen, I forgive you.

==

Oenone

RIVER, MY CHILD, GATHER THE threads of this. Although they bring pain, his final days are yours to hold too. They keep this complete, commit this to memory. Do not cut out and let fall away the pieces that do not make you smile. He let the light shine in through the open door onto his face and you must always do the same and tell it as it was. That way the future is the past, one and the same.

My child, on his last day Hector and I carried him to the sea on a stretcher made of poles and woven reeds. We lay Paris at the water's edge. The tidal water rose in inches to take back the coloured pebbles. His feet became wet as the waves reached him first with tentative fingers, then armfuls of itself. I tell Paris that he *is* my son that was taken by a snake. That the snake has come for him too. I went to the town, I confess to him now, to try to get *blind* medicine. To be sure nothing would save him. I know, he murmurs. Just as I sought out the *blind* nurse after my boy was bitten, I tell him.

Paris tries to speak. I wet his lips.

What was her name? he manages.

I speak the name *Helen*. I remember her face clearly. She was unable to save my son, I say, as I have been unable to save you. Helen grieved along with the rest of us—all crying as a single woman into the godless dark. She escaped the capital before the war, to save her own child that was deep in her belly. I thanked her with my heart. Her presence was a sign: that she wasn't able to save my son made me certain there was no other life ahead meant for him. I did no wrong. My son's story was always to have ended where it did, at the mouth of a snake. She and I were one then, and are one now again, at the same place.

Paris did not speak after that.

So my child, feel us there on the beach. We three are one. Feel him, his thoughts, desires, final words. *She touches my face, cool.* Yes, child, there. That is him, let him come to you. *Her fingers make the shape of my cheek, jaw, brow, and lip.* The sea rushes out and in. Feel him. *Water dampens my neck and is trickled onto my papery tongue, salt. Old books my father owned are being lifted off the shelf and read, his voice is alive again here in my ears. Ah, she coos.*

His brother Hector shifts his weight and lays

him down on the pebbles and sand, building his head up, his breathing light and occasional. *Then come the faces. First, those ancient but familiar, neighbours and teachers, fellow regular passengers on a train, classmates, then come distant cousins, my aunt Hesione, my father is leaving to go to work, I am treating patients in hospital, and last in a swoosh of hung washing and laughter, my mother's face is before me—I am a boy and she my known world.*

The faces continue. Guards long gone, fellow prisoners tortured or released, dead or escaped. Then come the villagers and their familiar ways. Lastly strangers come. Those I've never met, or was supposed to meet had I avoided capture. They draw close and fade back, my only chance to be with them, to see where I had not gone.

The last of them, she comes close, but instead drifts away before I can see the face. Carry my name forward, I call after her. I am Paris. I am left alone then, with the wind. I am on a beach and there is wind. I leave with the water and wind, you stay here, I say to no one. I will leave, you stay, stay. Say my name. Stay.

My child, you must let his journey come to its rest here, at the beach where he took his last breath, the sea at his waist, his *ghost* brother holding his back and head, me at his side touching his face as he became absent, breathing in short stutters, then no breaths, then a small one, then none, none, one, none, none, no more.

Let the funeral plans begin, for we shall celebrate the life of the great *blind* doctor Paris. He who served our people and witnessed our war, saw us at our worst, wearing our darkest mask, and forgave us nonetheless. Let the food be cooked and the wine be poured. Let the dresses be sewn and the ribbons be tied. Let his friends and former captors mingle and sing as one under the same stars, no longer together for war. There will be no pyre. Let the tide turn and bury him in its currents—as was his wish.

Give me his child who he held just yesterday, whose beating heart he listened to with his ear and smiled. Healthy, he said. River will live long, he said, and we will tell her his prophesy. So give me his baby girl and let me pull her to me, hot and wet, with my hands and let me feed her milk.

Let his story be passed from mouth to mouth all across this country. Drum beat to drum beat. Let the truth of him—the *blind* doctor who did not leave, did not shame, or blame, or maim—rain from the clouds and seep into the lakes and rivers, into the gills of fish, onto the hooks of fisherman, inside the mouths of our children. Let us all rise and accept his great goodness.

Let us cross what cannot be crossed. Let the sky be the sea. Let the reflection be the object itself. Let the music in the reeds be the wind, and the frightened animal separated from the herd be the hunter. Let the dirt take the tears into it and become fertile. Let the meal be hunger and let the eye be the ear. Let the cure be the curse.

My child, Paris is your story. He is his own evidence and defence. He is no more than what you have of him. He breathes only when you do. Therefore, my child do not let *Paris* be an unspoken name in the night, a young doctor in a photograph leaving for our faraway country. Memorize his writings, the story of his life that he wanted to leave behind. Find the people he wrote about and share his story with them. His is a story that is indistinguishable from your own. If he is ever searched for, let him not be a pencilled name on a list of missing foreigners, an illegible signature in a guest book at the Colonial Hotel. No, let his name be the sun, the sky, the food, and all that is good.

=====

Notes

The quotations are from: Ovid's *Heroides, XVII: Helen to Paris* (Translator, Harold Isbell); H.D.'s epic poem *Helen in Egypt,* Leuké, Book II [2]; and the final lines from Lord Tennyson's epyllion "The Death of Oenone."

The pronunciation of Oenone is: *ee noh nee.*

Acknowledgements

I acknowledge, and am grateful for, the financial support of the Ontario Arts Council and the Canada Council for the Arts.

My tenure as Writer in Residence at St. Mary's College of Maryland gave me the gift of time to work on this book. I am grateful to Ruth Feingold, Karen Leona Anderson, and Jerry Gabriel.

This story began as a sequence of poems. Adam Sol and Gordon Johnston separately made compelling arguments for a novel. I thank them both. To Dean Cooke, my deep appreciation for believing in this story.

My thanks to the following writers, friends, who read various drafts: Michelle Berry, Lorraine Brown, Dr. Anthony Jeffery, Jay Johnston, and J.C. Sutcliffe.

To my editor and friend Michael Holmes, to Emily Schultz, and the good people at ECW Press, thank you.

Finally, to my first reader, Wendy Morgan, and to our children, Thomas and Ivy, much love.

At ECW Press, we want you to enjoy this book in whatever format you like, whenever you like. Leave your print book at home and take the eBook to go! Purchase the print edition and receive the eBook free. Just send an email to ebook@ecwpress.com and include:

- the book title
- the name of the store where you purchased it
- your receipt number
- your preference of file type: PDF or ePub?

A real person will respond to your email with your eBook attached. And thanks for supporting an independently owned Canadian publisher with your purchase!

BEN
33292013596402
wpa
Bennett, Jonathan, 1970-
The colonial hotel